CRASH
GO THE CARS!

SMASH
GO THE SPEED RECORDS!

THE CANNONBALL
SEA-TO-SHINING-SEA
MEMORIAL TROPHY DASH!

The
fun-filled . . .
good-natured . . .
admittedly illegal . . .
thoroughly anti-Establishm[ent]
fight for the finish line!

THE CANNONBALL RUN

**A Novel By
Michael Avallone**

**Based on the Screenplay by
Brock Yates**

LEISURE BOOKS ✺ NEW YORK CITY

For Warren Kemmerling
and his Marianne,
a winning team in the Race called Marriage
on the Highway called Life, since the flag went up in 1957.
May the Finish Line never be in sight.

A·LEISURE BOOK

Published by

Nordon Publications, Inc.
Two Park Avenue
New York, N.Y. 10016

THE CANNONBALL

Sea-To-Shining-Sea Memorial Trophy Dash

The Entries:

J. J. MCCLURE,
VICTOR,
PAMELA GLOVER, AND
DR. NICHOLAS VAN HELSING *all aboard an outlaw ambulance*
SEYMOUR GOLDFARB JR. *a flashy Aston-Martin*
THE SHEIK *a white Rolls Royce*
THE SHEIK'S SISTER
BRADFORD COMPTON AND
SHAKEY FINCH *a Suzuki motorcycle*
JAMIE BLAKE AND
MORRIS FENDERBAUM *a red Ferrari 308 GTS*
MARCIE THATCHER AND
JILL RIVERS *a black Lamborghini*
ARTHUR J. HOYT *no wheels*
STAN AND DAVE *a gray stock car*
MAD DOG AND
BATMAN *a brown GMC pickup truck*
SUBARU RACING TEAM *a Subaru*
PETOSKI AND FRIEND *a brown GMC van*

—and there can only be one winning team.

PIT STOPS

—and away we go!

CHECK YOUR OIL

The Western landscape was vast, endless—a wasteland of gleaming earth interrupted only by the broad ribbon of highway stretching toward a distant horizon. The sun was twelve o'clock high, a facsimile of a golden orange lost in space.

A small, bullet-shaped, black automobile was rocketing along the straight line of roadway, its shrieking engine propelling the vehicle at a speed of better than one hundred and sixty miles per hour down the two-lane road.

Ahead loomed a standard road sign, the black letters proclaiming SPEED LIMIT 55. The nose of the black car suddenly dipped, exhaust yowling, as the driver down-shifted gears to brake to a sliding, perilous halt. Sand and rock fragments flew from beneath the abruptly halted wheels. The automobile was a shimmering black Lamborghini Countach, the world's fastest road car.

It was almost obscenely streamlined, decked out with odd-shaped wings, shining spoilers, and yawning air scoops. A beauty in any automotive league. But the stunning blonde who leaped from the low interior was no less an eye-catcher. She ran toward the solitary sign; designer jeans and a low-cut, V-necked blouse made her a vision to remember, too.

Wielding a spray can, in no time at all, she had spurted a large, wide, red 'X' across the warning message. As she sped back toward the Lamborghini, the distant moan of a police siren ploughed through the Western silence. But the sound only spurred the blonde on.

The Lamborghini crammed into gear, and leaped ahead like a released cannonball, accelerating at a rate that had to be seen to be believed. The police car, in hot pursuit, was no more than a dot on the horizon.

The black, bullet-shaped Lamborghini opened up, engine roaring, all systems go. The vehicle literally flew.

It was no race at all. No chase, no contest.

The awesome gap widened between the dark car and the police machine, and they became but two specks on the immense topography. Vanishing Americans.

The Cannonball. The Sea-To-Shining-Sea Memorial Trophy Dash. Since its inception in nineteen seventy-one, this fun-filled, good-natured, admittedly illegal, and thoroughly anti-establishment affair—with absolutely no rules or regulations—has been a race to remember. It all boils down to one point, one goal. Put simply, the team that makes it from Darien, Connecticut, to the finish line in Los Angeles in the shortest time, is the winner.

Theoretically, a driver can win the Trophy Dash without breaking the law. On one level, the Cannonball is making a statement about safe drivers, good cars, the fifty-five-mile speed limit and the interstate highway system: it isn't the speed that is the problem. It is careless drivers and bad equipment. In all previous five runs of the race, there has never been an accident or injury. When vehicles are driven as fast as they will be driven in the Cannonball, a driver has to have a safe car and be alert every second.

Still, there are always the dangers of collision, injury and death. After all, if a tire blows out and you're doing better than fifty-five miles an hour—more like, say, one hundred and fifty-five—it's Goodbye, Columbus, wouldn't you say?

The golden orange of the sun burned fiercely down on a landscape that once again belonged to the rabbits, toads and rattlers. As it always does, in the end.

* * *

Las Vegas lay glittering, noisy, raucous and troubled beneath a frowning Nevada sky. The gambling-and-girls oasis in the southeastern corner of the state was still and ever the magnet for anyone and everyone who wanted to make a fast buck, and the greatest of these by any standards was Fenderbaum—Morris Fenderbaum. A bantam-sized black man with a contentious chin that poked out at the world belligerently, Fenderbaum was thin as a pencil, and lithe and sprightly as any professional dancer. But Fenderbaum was a gambler, from *G* to *R*. He had been hooked in the long-ago by poverty and deprivation.

Now he was deep inside his favorite casino, in a large backroom that was a clutter of desks and milling people. Everybody seemed to be using a telephone, talking rapid-fire. At the rear, men scribbled numbers on an immense blackboard, the focus of the room's activity. Surrounded by the oddsmakers and the bankers, Fenderbaum felt at home with this strange breed of gamblers who will take your bet on anything from basketball to horse racing to tiddlywinks, establishing the spreads on every form of competition known to Mankind. And Womankind, too. Not the least of these was Jimmy the Greek, the famed oddsmakers who led all the rest in successful coverage of bets.

Fenderbaum paused below Jimmy the Greek, who, at the moment, was busily working at the huge toteboard chalking up the odds on a column of names headed by the title: CANNONBALL SEA-TO-SHINING-SEA MEMORIAL TROPHY DASH. There was a wall map of the United States to the left of the toteboard. Fenderbaum frowned.

"Hey, Greek. How you figuring odds on that weirdo race?"

The Greek did not turn around. "Ain't easy. Nonstop. Coast to coast. How you going to pick a favorite in a layout like that?"

Fenderbaum snorted. "Big deal. All you gotta do is drive steady, stay out of trouble and have a good cover."

The Greek turned around, amused and contemptuous.

"Hey, man, the record for this race stands at thirty-two hours and fifty-one minutes." He gestured at the large map. "That means you average over eighty-five mph with cops on your ass every inch of the way. Don't give me that shit about driving steady."

Still scornful, he turned back to the toteboard and below the listed names, he inserted: MORRIS FENDERBAUM, 850-1.

"That's a scream, Greek," Fenderbaum sneered. "Who writes your stuff, the Hillside Strangler? You wanna bet or run your mouth?"

The Greek looked stunned. "You serious? Most people push grocery carts faster than you drive."

"Bet or no bet?" Fenderbaum hurled the challenge.

"You in the Cannonball . . ." The Greek shook himself. "Hmmm. Serious money says you're a hundred to one."

"You got a bet, schmuck!" Fenderbaum was angry now. "Twenty big ones at your odds. This time I get revenge on you, you Greek tragedy!"

"Hey, I just make the odds. *You're* the one who laid all that money on Harold Stassen."

"Nobody's perfect," Fenderbaum agreed. "But this time I got you."

The Greek shrugged and then suddenly his demeanor changed. A tall man with his back to them caught his eye. The Greek tugged the newcomer's coattail and rumbled a welcome. "Well, well. Jamie Blake. You ran Formula One a few years back, right?"

The tall man was tiredly handsome, rumpled, with vestiges of good humor lining a tanned dark face that suggested a touch of the gypsy, and some very faded good times. Still, there was an air of fight and class in the indolent eyes.

"Yeah," Jamie Blake said, without inflection. "A couple of seasons in Grand Prix. The Indy, too. Then Daddy took my car keys away. Now, Chocolate Drop here makes me a proposition."

"What a shame." The Greek seemed struck by that and again turned on Morris Fenderbaum who was watching Jamie Blake with gleaming interest. "Okay, so you set me up, half-pint. So you ran in a ringer. I'll still take your bet. You know why? Because you could run three guys as good as Blake and your big mouth would still get you in trouble! You don't know when to shut up."

Morris Fenderbaum shrugged, his eyes still atwinkle. "Hey, Greek—I'm just taking this gland case along with me for insurance. My real teammate is God. You got that, you overstuffed Zorba? God is my co-pilot!"

Jimmy the Greek sighed and turned back to

the toteboard, chalk ready again. He began to scribble.

Morris Fenderbaum and Jamie Blake exchanged glances.

All about them, oddsmakers and customers continued their ritual: barking orders into telephones, chalking up words and erasing numbers. The rumble and the clutter of Las Vegas never sleeps because it doesn't know how.

"God is your co-pilot?" Jamie Blake echoed.

"Yeah," Morris Fenderbaum leered. "My co-pilot."

"Ain't but two seats in a Ferrari, small man."

Fenderbaum held up the Star of David on the golden chain around his neck. His dark face shone.

"Never mind. We got Religion on our side!"

* * *

The small, battered Honda Civic puffed past a long row of blank-faced concrete buildings in the ugly industrial park and came to a stop before the closed overhead door that announced to a waiting world: J. J. MC CLURE   LAND-SEA-AIR TRAVEL   WE DELIVER. The man who alighted from the vehicle was rotund, happy-faced and utterly childlike, as if laughter had found a home in his fleshy body. There was a little boy in the man that not even greasy work clothes could hide. One pudgy hand held aloft a brown-paper lunch bag.

Behind the overhead door, the revving of a racing engine could be heard. There was no mistaking the high-pitched screech of a powerful machine. The rotund man smiled and hurried inside.

The rakish snout of a racing Porsche shone in the morning sunlight. Abruptly, the engine shut down and the new silence was nearly as deafening as the racket had been.

A dark-eyed, masculinely handsome face loomed above the engine compartment, rising with an evident expression of disapproval. Not for the Porsche, though. It was directed at the rotund man, and the story a quick glance at the clock told. The man's full moustache twitched, a gesture of anger and affection. J. J. McClure had put up with Victor a long, long time. But not even being a great mechanic excused his sidekick in a crisis.

"Hey, man, you're two hours late. I need you! This fuel injection is driving me crazy."

"I'm really sorry, J. J., but one of my gerbils had an anxiety attack and ate his treadmill. I just couldn't leave until I settled him down. I didn't want him to feel underprivileged and unloved."

"Victor." J. J.'s patience was beautiful to behold. "They've got vets for that. We've got other things to worry about."

"Gerbils are a big responsibility," Victor declared with some asperity, managing to look hurt, also.

"I know that, Victor. I am not asking you to take your gerbils lightly. I am merely asking you to concentrate on this engine. Imagine that we have a little army of gerbils inside here and we want them to be able to run on their little treadmill just as fast as their little legs can carry them. Right?"

"That's really a nice way of putting it. It would be nice if they could share the credit in winning the Cannonball." Victor gave an expert tug to a spanner wrench in the offending area of the engine. "That would make it a real team effort—you, me, the gerbils and *him.*"

J. J. McClure turned forceful in an instant. *Him again!*

"Victor, don't start. I don't want to hear about *him.*"

"I just wanted you to know that he'll help you if you need him. That's all."

"Dammit, Victor, I don't want to know about that!"

"He really likes you, you know," Victor continued, unruffled.

J. J. sighed, smiled and then adopted a patronizing tone. "Victor, that *is* really good news. But if you can get this thing to run right—you and me, that is—we may not have to ask *him* to take time off from his busy schedule to help us. Now that makes sense, right?" He might have been talking to that little boy in Victor.

Victor's happy face assumed noble contours.

"He's never too busy for us. We're his favor-

19

ites. You just wait. He'll prove it!"

J. J. Mc Clure smiled helplessly. The same old silly song.

Lovable Victor, Mechanic First Class, was also as loony as a bedbug with that weird notion of his—

Well—it didn't matter. Nothing mattered—as long as they got the damn engine working properly and they won the Cannonball! With or without *his* help.

What a monkey to have on your back! Whether *he* was real or not.

Victor's magic hands had solved the fuel injection problem. They road-tested the Porsche that very afternoon.

On an open stretch of highway, streaking across the flatlands, engine wide open, J. J. Mc Clure was pushing the Porsche to the limit. The one-hundred-and-thirty mph pace was rapidly accelerating and there wasn't another buggy in sight. So far as they could see, anyway. J. J.'s handsome face bent to the wheel, was opening up all the way. A happy smile crinkled his full moustache. His heart was singing.

Victor's booming voice heralded success. ". . . one hundred and eighty-five—and as steady as a rock!"

"This thing's a sure winner," J. J. agreed. "Fifty-gallon auxiliary fuel tank, antiradar paint, radar jammer and detector, one-hundred-watt linear for the CB . . . how can we lose?"

The question, of course, was rhetorical as the

Porsche bulleted ahead, humming powerfully.

But the police had another answer lined up.

They were positioned behind the rise, the one that obscured them from the long stretch of roadway now dropping behind J. J. and Victor in the hurtling Porsche. A veritable knot of patrol cars lay waiting, lights flashing, squawk boxes reporting the speedster's progress. Every patrolman was fingering hardware; pistols, shotguns, riot guns glittered. The Porsche engine was screaming its closeness now. The Defenders of the Law tensed, alert and ready. The moment held.

And then the Porsche shot into view, rising like a sun over the Rockies. It crested the rise of the hill, the engine running too quickly. Suddenly, the car began to yaw to the left and right, twisting and turning furiously as J. J. fought the wheel. Victor hiked his eyebrows up, round eyes goggling. J. J. was braking heavy, trying to hold the wheels to the road. He couldn't. The Porsche's speed overshot the topography.

It plunged directly into the cluster of crowded police cars at a tremendous speed, leaping and bouncing and barging through the roadblock. Lawmen scattered like ants discovered at an overturned honey jar on a picnic. Victor shut his eyes and clasped his pudgy hands in prayer. J. J. stuck to the job and brought the crumpled Porsche to a smoking, lurching stop on the roadway ahead of the cop cars. Soon, everything on two legs was sprinting toward the newly created wreck.

J. J. slumped over the wheel, heart hammering, ashes in his mouth. The Porsche couldn't win anything now. Not even a soap box derby.

The very first policeman to arrive at the Porsche's smashed door was a giant of a man, carrying a dark .38. He was shaken and angry over his own near brush with death.

"All right, you crazy bastards!" he bellowed. "Out of that car! And quick!"

Victor leaped from the still-smoking wreck, bounding high. But it was a Victor beyond ordinary belief. Or reason.

He was wearing a cowled mask *à la* Captain Marvel. But this time the words 'Captain Chaos' were crudely embroidered across the forehead. A home-made cape was draped over his rounded shoulders. He stood tall and proud, the gleam of eagles in his eyes.

"Who," blurted the stunned cop, "the hell are you, masked man?"

"I am Captain Chaos," Victor declared majestically, "and this is my faithful companion, Cato!"

His pudgy forefinger pointed to the slumped and defeated. J. J. McClure still pinned behind the wheel of the Porsche.

J. J. rested his tousled head in his hands, the picture of resignation and humiliation. And trapped Mankind.

He was back again. Captain Chaos—Victor's nutty, dippy, altogether useless alter ego.

Suddenly, the Cannonball Trophy Dash,

22

Memorial or otherwise, seemed a remote and hopeless dream.

Geezis! How do you get rid of an alter ego?

* * *

It was the main street of a backwater town deep in the fabled Carolinas. A warm serenity seemed to drown care and strife in the pleasant atmosphere of the afternoon. But sliding around a street corner, a bulging, fat-tired stock car invaded the sleepy business district of the town. With spluttering, roaring noises, it tore along, a commotion altering irrevocably the tenor and tone of the day.

A slumbering police car roused to action, took off in pursuit, light flashing, siren howling. The stock car slowed; the cruiser urged it to the curb.

The cruiser cop, a pure redneck model with reflective sun-glasses and straw hat to match, ambled over to the fidgety pair. Leaning against the side of the stock car, he drawled, "You boys got a license for that thing?"

On the passenger side, Stan, a short, lean man, glanced at his partner. Then the pride of the Barrett family returned the policeman's smile.

"No, but we was fixin' to get one today. We was just on our way to the license bureau just when you stopped us."

The cop squinted in disbelief. "Well, get that damn thing off the streets before I run you both in." Off in the hazy blue, a jetliner thundered.

David Pearson, the tall and burly driver, protested. "But we got to test it out someplace!"

The cop smiled knowingly, almost kindly. "You boys still gonna run in that crazy race?"

Stan shook his head. "Not unless we can test it out a little bit." His voice held a near-whine of supplication.

The cop's oily smile disappeared. He poked an irate thumb in their direction. "Well, not on the damn streets in the damn middle of the damn town! And I'll tell you boys another thing." He paused and glanced around the vacant intersection. His voice dropped confidentially. "If'n you want to get anywhere in that Cannonball thing, I'd get me a paintbrush and cover over those numbers on the doors!"

Stan Barrett and David Pearson followed his thumb and gazed in dawning wonder at the large racing numbers dominating the door panels of their favorite red stock car, a veritable advertisement of their intentions.

David nodded quickly. "By golly, I believe you've got something there. Indeed I do—"

Stan chuckled appreciatively. "We'll take care of that right away, and we sure do cotton to your help, *Uncle Domer.*"

Officer Domer, redneck getting redder, growled benignly and climbed back into his cruiser. Stan Barrett and David Pearson watched him go with dawning respect. At least the old redneck was good for something!

He had given them a great piece of advice, that is, if they had any real ideas about winning the Cannonball!

God bless the old turkey!

* * *

Lovely green vistas, as far as the eye could see, surrounded the classic Beverly Hills mansion of the Goldfarb dynasty. The setting had all the luscious, bucolic serenity of a Gainsborough landscape. And one half-expected the flashy Aston-Martin DB-6 coupe that came into view, slithering along the long, winding driveway up to the gates of the manor. The vehicle was a silver dream, the best that lots of money—and good taste—could buy. Its very sleekness gave an ominous aspect to the Aston-Martin but if anything this increased the glamor and suitability.

The operator of the vehicle was tall, handsome, and impeccably attired in striking synchrony with his car. This was no less than Seymour Goldfarb, the heir to millions. A liveried butler greeted this sartorial apotheosis as he stepped from his car and mounted the low, wide, stone steps of the main entrance. For the umpteenth time, the servant marvelled that his master was the spitting image, dead ringer and all-around duplicate of Roger Moore. In fact, the master might very well have stepped out of a James Bond movie. From shining shoes to smooth-haired head, he was perfect casting. In fact, the arch-villains of Ian Fleming's novels—Blofeld, Dr. No, Goldfinger and Mr. Big—would have shot him on sight.

Seymour Goldfarb strolled indolently through the main hall into the lavish drawing room where his elderly mother was quietly practicing her afternoon ritual of tea and crumpets. The butler bowed slightly and withdrew. Seymour Goldfarb draped his tall, elegant figure across a comfortable chair. Roger Moore could not have done it any better. Seymour Goldfarb was a *compleat* reincarnation of the screen matinée idol, down to the mole on the cheek.

"Well, Mother dear." Seymour Goldfarb soothed her in an exquisitely accented voice. "I trust your day has been pleasant."

His mother, every inch the *grande dame,* winced visibly as she set down her teacup. The Jewish *grande dame.*

"A nightmare," she murmured. "A living nightmare. You are killing me, Seymour. Killing me a slow death with this idiot spy business."

"But Mother, I don't understand . . ." Beguiling innocence wreathed her son's handsome face.

"What's to understand?" Mother Goldfarb's voice rose. "I am looking at my son, Seymour Goldfarb Jr., son of Seymour Goldfarb—God rest his soul—and heir to the largest ladies' ready-to-wear business west of the Rockies, and what is he doing? Walking around acting like he's some *goy* movie actor named Roger Moore."

Seymour Goldfarb raised his carefully plucked eyebrows.

His mother shuddered. "For this I sent you to the best schools? For this, I'm spending eight thousand in orthodonture work? For this I am going broke paying that Wilshire Boulevard analyst?"

Her gorgeous son was unruffled. Smiling, he shrugged. "Really, Mother." He purred in protest. "It's much more complicated than that."

"Don't tell me from complicated!" his mother roared back. "What about this? The live-in maid found it under your pillow this morning."

She had magically produced a Beretta 7.65 mm automatic pistol from the folds of her lap. The perfect James Bond weapon.

Seymour Goldfarb's eyes went cold. His smooth face hardened into an icy mask. His tone, when he replied, was accusing.

"Mother, I must insist you stay out of my personal affairs."

"My only son! With a pistol! A homicidal maniac yet. Where did I go wrong?" The question was hurled to the sky, to the Gods. Mrs. Seymour Goldfarb wailed pitifully, wrung her hands. Her tea, forgotten, had gone cold.

Seymour Goldfarb had retrieved the pistol from her as soon as she had shown it. He spun it deftly until it lay coiled very easily in the palm of his hand.

"I'm awfully sorry about this, Mother," he said in a bland yet flat and deadly tone. "Although I expect you're going to regret it more than I." The nose of the Beretta rose menacingly as Seymour Goldfarb stood before her like the Angel of Death. Or James Bond. Like everything else in life, it depends upon your point of view.

"Seymour! Put that thing down—"

Her eyes were wide with shock, terror, the unreality.

"I'm terribly sorry, Mother," Seymour Goldfarb said in a dead monotone. "But you know too much already. In the business I'm in, even the deepest family relationships don't count a farthing."

"Farthing?" was the echoing wail of Mother Goldfarb. "What's from a farthing? Twenty-one thousand for your Bar Mitzvah alone! Don't that count for something?"

Seymour Goldfarb's Double-Oh-Seven eyes were merciless. Set. Decided. His finger tightened on the trigger of the Beretta.

"Goodbye, Mother," he said.

Mother Goldfarb screamed in horror and flung her hands over her face.

The pistol roared with a splat of sound, recoiled in the palm of Seymour Goldfarb's hand. It was done. His victim lay slumped awkwardly; the half-empty teacup rattled helplessly. Remorse flickered across his face as he gazed at the barrel of the gun. A small red flag protruded from the muzzle, waving gracefully in the faint turbulence, the last ripple of the explosion. On the red flag was the black printed legend: BANG!

Seymour Goldfarb had killed his loving mother the only way he knew how.

* * *

The gas station attendant was thoroughly baffled.

The brown GMC van parked between his six pumps had no less than that many hoses plugged into its broad flanks. And all were going like sixty. Meters madly clicked off gallons of gasoline—51, 52, 53, 54. . . . It was unbelievable. But not much less believable than the van itself.

Painted on its high sides, in large letters, were the words POLISH RACING DRIVERS OF AMERICA. The special PRDA emblem gleamed like a special kind of medal. Or even a memorial.

The driver of the van, a loose-jointed blond, was checking the pumps. The PRDA emblem was repeated on his crew-neck shirt. The young, hippy-dippy gas attendant had never quite seen anyone like Petoski. He was one of a kind.

When the furious clicking stopped, he pulled all the pumps, returning them to their brackets. The attendant marveled anew: Petoski was flashing a roll of bills that would choke a horse.

"Lemme see, how much do I owe you?"

"I don't believe this." The attendant gulped.

"Don't try. It'll only give you bad dreams."

"The way I add it up, it's three hundred and forty-five gallons. That's . . . let's see—" The attendant was awed. "Geezis! That's four hundred and forty-eight—fifty!"

Petoski peeled quickly from the green roll of bills. "Here's five hundred. Keep the change."

"Hey, man, thanks! But lemme ask you something. Er—what are you going to do, I mean, why are you carrying all that gas?"

Petoski looked determined, his small eyes glinted. "Well, we're planning a little trip to California. That is, if we can find it." He jerked a thumb at his partner in the van.

"What do you mean, find it?"

"California," Petoski repeated grimly.

The attendant's glance flicked automatically to the Polish emblem on the truck. "Find California?" he echoed.

"Yeah." Petoski elaborated, "We've never been there before. It might be kind of hard to find."

The attendant glanced again at the Polish logo on the van. A faint smile dawned, a smile that vanished as Petoski laid a giant hand on his shoulder.

"Hey, Jack, don't even *think* it."

"Hey, man," the attendant was suddenly earnest now. "It's—uh—easy to find California. Just go down here—" he pointed down

30

the roadway, "—hook a left. It's about three thousand miles. You can't miss it."

Even as the brown GMC van pulled away from the station, with its incredible gasoline cargo, the attendant was still shaking his head. The young attendant could not know that the famed Cannonball Memorial Trophy Dash was drawing them all. Every kind of driver—like bees to honey, like a starving, thirsty man to meat and drink; for the race was not only to the swift. It was to everyone who could get into it, including the Polish Racing Drivers of America.

Bless them all.

FILL 'ER UP!

The aircraft was a twin-engine Helio Courier
STOL, and J. J. was doing the flying, his Victor
on look-out. Neither of the two, however, despite
the brightness of the day and the warmth of the
sun, was thinking much about anything but the
Cannonball. Especially J. J. That handsome
worthy, who wore his masculinity so easily and
unawares, was nearly beside himself with trying
to think of a way out of their dilemma.

"This is one delivery job I don't need," J. J.
was grumbling, and then pausing, he muttered
to himself. "How about a limousine with
diplomatic plates?" He brightened rapidly and
turned to Victor. "How about a bloodmobile?
They'd never stop *that*."

The Courier hummed vibrantly. J. J. reached
behind the cockpit and came up with a can of
beer. He shook it unhappily. It was empty—just
like Victor's head, sometimes.

"Aw, terrific. Now we're out of beer. How
can my quick wit and razor-sharp reflexes
operate without beer?"

Victor was worried. "You gotta take it easy,

J. J. This Cannonball thing is making you crazy."

J. J. looked eastward. His eyes riveted on something far below them, and he pushed forward on the stick.

"Easy for you to say. Less than a month to go and we still don't have a car."

Victor agreed, meek and subdued. "And no license either."

"Yeah. Thanks to *him*."

"Easy now," Victor cautioned. "You know he's very thin-skinned. We mustn't hurt his feelings."

"Dune buggy . . ." J. J. was groping for inspiration once more. "That might work . . . run it cross-country . . . Straight line, coast to coast. Or a Trailways bus . . . or an armored personnel carrier. . . . Yeah! Let 'em try to stop that!"

Victor was looking out the plexiglas window, alarmed. "You better pay attention, J. J. This looks tricky."

J. J. was definitely not listening. ". . . a New York taxi . . . a garbage truck . . ."

"Easy, J. J."

". . . a Brink's truck . . ."

The possibilities were endless as to what types of vehicle could run the Cannonball, undetected by the law and the competition. The more immediate problem at hand was setting down the aircraft. But still there was a lot to think about. Too much.

First, there was the matter of a vehicle now

that the Porsche had been knocked out of the box—thanks to the wreck and the police. And then, of course, there was Victor. Dear, sweet, light-headed Victor and his troublesome alter ego, Captain Chaos.

Victor wasn't just a mechanics wizard. No, he was more than that. The pudgy sidekick was like a brother to J. J., whose own family was gone. J. J. was all Victor had in the world, and J. J. had come to regard the roly-poly mechanic as the one person in the whole wide world who really needed him. That was important to J. J., someone to care about, think about. There was no Miss Right, yet. Oh, there had been plenty of dames, all right. J. J. was easy to love, easy to have a good time with. But there was no one permanent, yet.

So J. J. had sort of made Victor his responsibility. Taking care of the childlike fat man had come to be a way of life for him. And that meant taking care of Captain Chaos too, as much of a pain as 'he' could be at times. But Victor was perfectly harmless. He was not crazy—just a pixie. And both J. J. and Victor had the same unrelenting, unchanging love of engines and speed and automobiles. It was their whole life, and something they shared together.

Problem One, *now,* though, was how to get a vehicle for the Cannonball. It had to be a fast machine that would escape detection, for they were going to have to travel through a lot of states at better than fifty-five miles per hour. and that was going to take some doing. But what kind of vehicle would fool the cops and pass inspection?

J. J. sighed, eyes still searching, and concentrated on the twin-engine Helio Courier STOL. They had to set down soon.

With lowered landing gear, flaps down, feathered props, J. J. sought a landing. The aircraft slid forward on a long gliding run that skimmed treetops and made life far too interesting for Victor, who closed his eyes again.

J. J. was making a perfectly routine landing except that he was landing on the main street of a small, typical American town. A Norman Rockwell burgh, revisited, with rows of white, clapboard houses, and a pristine church spire that rose above billowing maple and elm trees. J. J. yanked a throttle and taxied calmly into the parking lot of a 7-Eleven store. As if prearranged, Victor leaped out of the plane and ran into the store, scuttling like a crab. J. J. rubbed his eyes tiredly, still pondering ways and means of entering the Cannonball. His imagination had just about run dry.

Meanwhile, in the store, Victor was loading up for his friend and companion, six-packs the order of the day.

A pasty-faced, gum-chewing girl watched him with an idle interest, but only because he was the sole moving object in the store. She had barely batted an eye at the sight of an airplane camped practically on her front stoop.

Victor paid for the beer, managing a foolish smile, and turned to leave as quickly as he had come in. Unfortunately, by this time, J. J. had rotated the plane. Unfortunately, the front door of the store lay directly in the prop-wash of the sitting Courier STOL. As Victor swung open the door, all hell broke loose.

An enormous blast of air funneled directly into the heart of the 7-Eleven. It left nothing but destruction in its awful wake.

Victor was blown into the counter, and held on for dear life to keep the windstream from sending him aloft like a toy balloon. His eyes bulged, his body shook, but he never let go of the six-pack. J. J. would never have forgiven him.

The horrifying tempest unleashed—innocently and accidentally—a flying catastrophe of newspapers, magazines, soup packets—the instant kind—tea bags, pantyhose, razor blades, film cartons, potato chips, candy bars, key chains; and the entire universe of packaged merchandise glided, flung, swirled, eddied and whipped about the confines of the store. Even as Victor pried himself away from the counter and loped toward the plane, the pasty-faced counter girl chewed her gum in disdain and rolled her eyes toward the heavens in complete lack of concern. The 7-Eleven was a shambles now, looking like one of those paperweights one shook violently to set a mini-snowstorm in motion.

The chaos in the heart of the 7-Eleven was indeed something to write home about. Or tell the kids. But outside it was the same story. In any case, it was to become history and legend in the annals of this little picture-pretty town. For the Courier, with its propellor still whirling, had set the main street in a muddled uproar. Cars skidded, others braked wildly, all to avoid hitting the bright red aircraft squatting in the center of the thoroughfare. Bicyclists lay sprawled, onlookers gesticulated or stood in frozen amazement, while others ran to see what all the fuss was about. A stout policeman, shrilling his whistle, was already on the dead run, trying to thread a path between jammed autos and conveyances. But, waiting for his pudgy pal and his desired beer, J. J. McClure literally yawned through it all.

With Victor steeling himself by his side, J. J. finally sprang into action, hurling the Courier aloft. Using the main street freely for takeoff, he narrowly missed a Pinto, blithely steered by an old lady who had seen too many years to be disturbed by anything new. The Courier clawed for the skies, thundering as it soared. The crowd below shook a collective fist.

J. J. McClure broke the tension with a *Whoop!*, his voice filled with glee and the thrill of solution and discovery. "I got it! A hearse with a blown Hemi! And we could use the casket as an extra fuel tank!"

Victor, fumbling with the six-pack, winced. He was still breathing hard. "That's pretty weird, J. J. Maybe you ought to see somebody. Get some help, you know what I mean?"

J. J. McClure hardly heard the words, much

less the concern in Victor's voice. He was still only thinking, Cannonball, Cannonball. . . .

Cannonball! The only race that meant a damn thing. He had to calculate all the ways of getting into this biggest contest, the Great Race, the Memorial Dash Trophy gig. And the means—don't forget the means. They add up to everything.

* * *

The Wind Tunnel Test Facility was a beehive of activity, a perfect setting for plans, organization and purpose of a high order.

A group of white-smocked Japanese engineers were flocking about a rakish sportscar, a gleaming, streamlined beauty of a Subaru. Behind them, a mob of Japanese businessmen, all carrying Nikon cameras, were dutifully watching the engineers do their technical stuff. Inside the car, banks of computers and blinking instruments were operating at high peak. The engineers made notes and compilations on legal-size yellow pads. The businessmen nodded their approval and reached for their Nikons. All great moments should be recorded on film, particularly the glowing achievements of Japanese automotive technology.

Nearby, trying to retain their Oriental impassivity, a team of drivers in perfectly tailored, matching white overalls, looked on. The car's computers whirred and clicked. The technicians and the executives were jabbering excitedly now.

The First Driver nodded vigorously and spoke over the commotion to Driver Number Two, his honorable colleague, in words to this effect:

"Goddamn, you-all. When them redneck mothers see this little hunk of iron, they gonna think they got ass-kicked by a Brahma bull!"

Driver Number Two could not have agreed more. Still—he showed his perfect teeth in a smile and replied: *"You never can trust these technical bastards. They don't have to drive what they invent."*

"Don't lose any sleep over this baby. It'll make anything on wheels eat dust."

"I'm with you, Boo-Boo. Don't forget to bring plenty of tapes. Rock and country. I'll bring the movies."

Driver Number One nodded and watched a fat businessman step in closer with his Nikon to snap the dashboard of the Subaru. He tried not to shake his head. One must never show disapproval before one's superiors. He kept his face placid, but tight-lipped, out of the side of his mouth said: *"Look at that fat bastard."*

"Better keep it to yourself."

"Oh? Why?"

"That is Noyama," Driver Number Two said. *"He pays our salaries."*

Just then, Mr. Noyama-San backed out of the car and glanced at the drivers with a frown. Driver Number One grinned sheepishly and waved a thumbs-up. *"Ride 'em high!"* he yelled.

Driver Number Two murmured impatiently, *"Let's get this show on the road."*

"Yeah," the other driver agreed. *"Sure want to see the good ole U.S. of A. again."*

"You have relatives there?"

"Hell no! It's the dames. They're gorgeous in America. They all wear jeans now. All the time. Murder."

Cameras continued to click away, like exclamation points to the excited chatter of the assorted businessmen and technicians. The Subaru sparkled like a gem.

Driver Number Two bowed. *"I hear you talking, Gate Mouth."*

All in all, another strange entry for the Cannonball—made in Japan.

* * *

The low-slung powerboat, under an expert hand, cut a determined path toward an invisible destination.

The marina channel was choppy and unsettled. In spite of a high wind that was hitting the off-shore tide, the overhead sun beat down as if J. J. McClure and Victor were two eggs in need of frying. Combatting this assault, J. J. wore a flopping straw hat, but no shirt. Victor was about to bust a gut leaning over an open engine hatch at the stern, plying his technical know-how. The wake of the boat created countercurrent that heaved passing sailboats and smaller craft against the pilings of the dock. J. J. was oblivious to all, his mind still locked into the contemplation of ways and means. A legion of furious sailors was gathering on the docks of the soaked marina, in protest of the speeding boat.

". . . then we could always go with a nice plain Chevy sedan," mused J. J., ". . . with a trunk full of Sidewinder missiles. . . ."

Victor glanced astern and blanched. "Hey, J. J.. . . . maybe we ought to back it down a little?"

"Look," J. J. snapped angrily. "I ain't spending the rest of my life delivering this sled! We gotta be in time for the Cannonball —right? Damn sure tootin'!"

The powerboat swept past a party junk, one of those be-flagged, bedecked pleasure boats loaded to the gunwales with what J. J. and the rest of the male world considers foxy girls. They were enough to distract J. J. momentarily. He waved and grinned broadly with instant approval.

Victor, still worried about their stern and what might be behind them, was shielding his eyes in the time-honored nautical gesture. "I think the harbor patrol is after us. I think maybe it is the Coast Guard."

J. J. whirled at that, shaking head. "What? I can't hear you."

"The Coast Guard," Victor howled. "The

Coast Guard!"

"What the hell has the Coast Guard got to do with the Cannonball?"

The foxy ladies were still waving, still expressing their interest, still showing bouncing breasts, white teeth and flashing smiles. J. J. leered back at them. Now, he gallantly waved his straw hat, one hand on the powerboat wheel.

He was happy, unsuspecting. Unafraid.

He didn't see the houseboat dead ahead. Not until he turned away from the foxy crew. Then there it was, bigger than the Rock of Gibraltar, bigger than Texas.

He spun the wheel, his heart stopping. He cried out, Victor in chorus. That, of course, stopped nothing.

Terrified passengers were leaping madly from both sides of the houseboat to get out of harm's way while they still had a chance. A boat whistle shrilled deafeningly. J. J.'s eyes bulged with horror. The powerboat nosed directly into the houseboat, like a shark coming in for a kill. *Jaws Three!*

The world exploded.

After that—nothing.

When J. J. McClure opened his eyes once again, it was to find himself, recumbent, on the strapped cot of a vehicle grinding along at top speed. And across from him, in similar condition, was good old Victor.

Both of them were noticeably drenched. Victor was not visibly hurt, but seemed to be in great pain, as evidenced by the rolling of his two black-marble eyes. J. J. felt himself all over gingerly. There was a bandage of alarming thickness over his forehead. Geezis.

"Hey, J. J.—" Victor's voice was a squeak from the big body.

"You gonna make it, Victor?"

"Not if I hang around you much longer."

"Aw, shit," sighed J. J. "Nobody's perfect."

Victor moaned a little before crying out to the attendant that hunched between them in the aisle of the ambulance. "Make sure we don't get a double room. This maniac is trying to kill me." A grimace contorted his fat face. "By the way, how much longer to the hospital?"

The attendant smiled a patient grin. "We'll be there in a couple of minutes. We can smoke through the traffic like shit through a goose in this thing."

The white ambulance, true to his estimate, rocketed and streaked through the streets. All other vehicles veered to the curb, acknowledging its right of way. J. J. McClure was hit by a sudden bolt of mental lightning.

He sat up on the cot, heedless of his injuries and lifted the swathing bandage that had slipped over his eyes. He looked across the aisle at Victor, back out at the traffic parting before the emergency vehicle like the Red Sea under the wand of Moses, and then again at Victor. An expression of wild satisfaction began to light his darkly handsome face, and he began to laugh.

The answer to all his problems, and Victor's,

had been provided—he was riding in it, right now.

Of course! The perfect disguise, the greatest cover of all.

Certainly! Nobody would ever look twice at an ambulance.

Natch! Everything on the road would move out of the way.

It was all so beautifully simple, so damn apparent, he was surprised at himself for not seeing it sooner.

* * *

In the Middle Eastern stretches on the far side of the world, on a vast and sandy landscape older than Time itself, two camel-mounted Bedouin tribesman were witnessing something that was not exactly the workings of the All and Powerful Allah. Indeed, what exactly was transpiring before their eyes almost defied the prophets and all the words and wisdom of the Wise Ones.

The tribesmen, decked out in flowing *burnooses,* mocassin-shod feet, bandoliers of bullets and long, engraved rifles, could scarcely credit their eyes. It was not the incongruous technology—oil wells towering over endless dunes—a familiar sight by now. What challenged their credibility was the immense white

Rolls Royce zooming along the narrow, sand-swept road.

By the Prophet!

The son of the Desert, Heir to the Treasuries of Araby, was eating up the very land itself with his scorchingly fast vehicle.

One of the Bedouins sighed. "The young Sheik fancies himself a racing driver."

His companion grunted and showed white teeth in a fiercely bearded face. The blowing sand pattered around his eyes. "I wouldn't let that little squirt drive my goats around the oasis."

Nobody likes a fool. Even a rich one. The tribesmen turned away, leaving the majestic Rolls Royce to conquer the desert. As it thundered over knolls and rising hillocks of earth in its flaming passage toward the palace, all within viewing distance shook their heads and galloped out of the path of the vehicle. The young Sheik was insane for speed.

Soon, the sandy desert was left behind. More oil wells and the flames of a refinery cat-cracker curled up toward the azure, cloudless skies. A broad promenade loomed against the arabesqued windows and arches of the turreted palace. Near the circular driveway, an old man tended a herd of goats, urging them onward. They scattered as the white Rolls Royce sped onto the promenade. At the far end, decked out in flowing robes of great delicacy and richness, sat a figure evidently plying needle and thread in embroidery of some kind.

The smoking limousine halted at last, with a stilling of its great motor, and from its depths emerged a young Sheik, his dark complexion sharply contrasting against the white robes that billowed around his body. Ludicrous wire-rimmed sunglasses were the only detail that marred the otherwise quintessential portrait of an Arab Sheik, with the falconlike nose, the black moustache and even blacker goatee.

Out of the back seat spilled two bodyguards, huge musclemen in black business suits with massive bulges at their left breasts signaling the presence of firearms. They were still shaking from their latest suffering of the driving techniques of their young lord and master who stalked away from them imperiously. Who would guard the bodyguards? They turned their backs and furtively crossed themselves, as though Allah alone was not big enough for the job.

The robed woman seated at the marble mosaic table did not turn around at the noise of the Rolls. In fact, she continued what she was doing unabated. Even when the young daredevil took a chair across from her, picked up a copy of the *London Financial Times* and began to read, she hardly stirred.

Now, two quiet servants materialized from nowhere with a large bowl of assorted fruit and a curious drink that resembled one of those weird concoctions one might see at *Trader Vic's,* thoroughly Americanized, passing for something Far Eastern or Polynesian. The servants withdrew as silently as they had come.

At this point, the woman spun in her chair and it was readily apparent that, rather than embroidery or needlework of any kind, she had been busy with a fine game of double solitaire. More striking than that was the woman's bare face, free of the traditional veil that ordinarily covered the female features. Her own features were richly, artfully made up in the longed-for, and classic *Vogue* style.

The woman, by any standards, was a kooky knockout, with heavily lipsticked mouth like a red gash, and eyes bright and garish with plucked, winged black eyebrows. A golden cigarette holder dangled from the red lips, blue smoke curled lazily upward.

The woman now spoke and, like all the rest of her, it did not fit at all. Her accent was clipped, British.

"How goes your driving, my brother?" The woman lay down the king of diamonds on a red queen.

"Allah now be praised, dear sister." The young Sheik's brassy voice was nonetheless tinged with Arabia. "My speed is rivaled only by the lightning bolts from the heavens."

"Do you still intend to enter this race with infidel Americans?"

The young Sheik raised his dark eyes skyward. His goatee twitched. "The Cannonball will fall to the forces of Islam, dear sister. I pledge it."

He walked over to his exotic sister and slapped a black ten of clubs triumphantly over a red nine of hearts.

These were but two more weirdos, as J. J. McClure would most certainly call them, intent on entering the Cannonball Memorial Trophy Dash . . . the Sea-to-Shining-Sea all-out affair that was attracting everyone and everything on wheels. Any kind of wheels.

* * *

In the interior of a large cargo aircraft winging its way over the United States, Mr. Bradford W. Compton was seated on a Harley-Davidson affair of fine lineage. Compton was dressed in a clean-cut dark serge business suit and comforting himself with a sip of what had to be a martini. Bradford W. Compton, the chairman of more companies than even he could tally, was a very serious and astute sort of person. He was tall, fairly young still, the bushy fullness of his dark hair topping a rather attractive male face. Not so the man seated across from him in the big cargo ship. Arthur Rose, his personal manager, was smallish, haggard-looking and altogether a worrier, with a voice that needed lots of oiling. Wall Street stockbroker and magazine publisher Bradford W. Compton, for all his brilliance, left small details to his underlings. And sometimes that could be costly.

Compton eyed the little man carelessly.

"You'll have the car waiting, is that correct?"

"Of course, Mr. Compton."

"And don't forget to cancel the board meeting on Monday. I'm going to take a week in Spain. At the castle."

"Of course, sir."

"And Arthur, you must locate that old friend of mine, Shakey Finch. He is the best long-distance motorcycle rider in the nation. Do you understand that?"

"Yes, sir." His voice rasped more than ever.

Bradford W. Compton reached for the shining crash helmet. When everything was ready, he hunched over the handlebars of his boldly colored bike, looking extremely purposeful. Arthur Rose restrained a shudder and grabbed him by the arm, suddenly.

"Mr. Compton, the Board has asked me to convey their concern about this one more time. Please reconsider . . ."

"Not possible, Arthur. They will simply have to permit me this one little indulgence to my ego."

Arthur Rose subsided, defeated once more.

No one argued with Success, and Bradford W. Compton had never been anything less than successful in all that he said or did.

The door of the cargo plane was now open.

Compton throttled the bike handles, started off with a racketing roar of sound, deafening within the confines of the plane. With a thrust and a spurt, he nosed through the open door and was gone. Arthur Rose could not bear to look.

But still seated on the motorcycle, serenely in the hands of his destiny, as well as the laws of gravity, Bradford W. Compton was tumbling earthward, falling, falling, falling. Black smoke was billowing from the bike's exhaust pipes, trailing his passage all the way down to Mother Earth, a free-fall of incredible dimensions. *And* statistics. Worthy perhaps of an Evel Knievel.

Suddenly, release. Compton was gone from the motorcycle, a parachute flashing behind him. The bike plummeted downward, beating out its former occupant to the greensward. There was a violent explosion, a burst of flame and noise. Compton drifted earthward, calm, cool and collected.

A small knot of men, women and children down there on *terra firma* had witnessed the whole thing. One simple-looking, middle-aged man wearing a 'Cat' diesel hat and bib overalls clapped his hands in wild approval of Compton's heroics.

His lady, a dour female in curlers, was unamused by it all. Viewing the scene through bejeweled aluminum sunglasses, she watched as Bradford W. Compton came in for a perfect landing. She snorted and said in a bored monotone, "That's the dumbest thing I've *ever* seen since that banana tried to jump the Snake River Canyon."

Bradford W. Compton could not have cared less, for he had completed the first labor of his journey, the journey that would lead him to the

Cannonball.

Which also made him but one more for the race.

* * *

Darien, Connecticut is a tweedy type of town but it is metropolitan all the same, like any other New York suburb. You will find well-turned-out housewives scuttling along along in their Volkswagens and Mercedes while 10-speed bicycles skim along the curbs. But sometimes in the midst of all this predictable scenery and citizen movement, you can see the unusual. Today, in this case, an elegantly painted GMC truck, the pickup kind. And in this vehicle were two types of men also not normally seen on the streets of Darien, Connecticut. The names alone—Mad Dog and Batman—would certify their strangeness and uncommonness.

Driving was a lean, black man in his early thirties. This was Mad Dog. Batman was beside him, a laconic Westerner slouching in his seat with scuffed cowboy boots hiked up carelessly on the dashboard. They chugged through traffic, as if they had all the time in the universe, to the hammering of a violent trucking tune. They surveyed their surroundings without much enthusiasm. Darien was far too square.

"Damn," Mad Dog snarled. "I never will

know how these Easterners stand living like this. Look at 'em.''

"All jammed up like a bunch of damn cattle in a stockyard," opined Batman, hunching his shoulders. The setting chilled him.

"It's like Race Day every day."

"I hope you're right about the Speedway not minding us borrowing their truck for a few days."

Mad Dog jerked his head.

"Hell, think of the publicity we'll get if we win. I can see the headlines: *Indianapolis Motor Speedway Employees Win Cannonball Cross-Country Race!* We'll be heroes."

"And if we lose," Batman added dryly, "I can see the poster in the post office . . . *Wanted for interstate grand larceny and car theft—Shoot!*"

Mad Dog stirred suddenly. His black face crinkled.

"Oh, oh. Look at that."

An old, noisy, blue Berlinetta Ferrari, a white ambulance and a red Porsche 930 Turbo Jet shot past in the opposite direction, an odd mixture in any motorized league. Mad Dog blasted the GMC horn, breaking the otherwise tranquil scene. The faces of J. J. McClure and Victor at the wheel of the ambulance had meant nothing to him.

Batman straightened erect, boots clumping to the floorboards. "You know them boys, Mad Dog?"

"Not hardly. I just figured they're Cannonballers. With all the special headlights, out-of-state plates and all. Yep—" Mad Dog smiled in satisfaction. "They're Cannonballers, all right!"

"They was going in the opposite direction. You think they know where the motel is?"

"It's supposed to be down here somewhere but I'm getting plenty tired of looking. If there's one thing that makes me crazy, it's circling around town looking for some damn motel!"

Mad Dog, impatient with the slow-moving traffic, yanked the horn lanyard again and set off a tremendous blast of sound as a WASP little Darien housewife in a pink Subaru blocked his path. The fancy-painted GMC truck bypassed her, swung about and headed in the direction the ambulance, Porsche and Ferrari had taken. Mad Dog and Batman fell into line, two more yo-yos for the Cannonball.

The entrants were piling up, their destination *Ye Olde English Inne*. Double-billed on its marquee were two conflicting greetings:

WELCOME, CANNONBALLERS!
as well as
WELCOME, FRIENDS OF NATURE.

The Fairfield County Chapter of the Friends of Nature was now in session, its annual strategy meeting that had nothing at all to do with the running of the Cannonball Memorial Trophy Dash.

Until now, as it was to turn out. J. J. McClure, in particular, was in for a date with Destiny—Destiny in the shape of a figure to set your clock by, sporting enormous sunglasses, long, blond hair and a sunny smile.

And she would go by the name of Pamela Glover, a lover of, among other things, trees.

TURN 'EM OVER

In the interior of the staid Ye Olde English Inne, the Chairperson of the Fairfield County Chapter of the Friends of Nature had risen to her feet to address her large audience. The Chairperson was female, humorless, with a face utterly devoid of makeup, her innate prettiness sadly defeated by a severe hairdo. Eyeglasses completed the portrait of *Don't-Treat-Me-Like-A-Woman*. She usually got exactly what she most derisively scorned: male interest and attention. In any case, she was now addressing the floor.

"Before we get to the speaker of the day, I'd like to thank Mona Corson of Westport for that lovely luncheon of hemp sandwiches and wood chip *consommé* . . ."

Loud applause thundered in the motel's large conference room, which was bursting with the Friends of Nature members. These consisted of young, bearded men with ponytails and small nylon knapsacks on their backs; skinny women in waffle-stompers and T-shirts emblazoned with such slogans as SAVE THE NEWTS and HAVE YOU HUGGED A PLANT TODAY?; well-dressed suburban clubwomen; graying, middle-aged men with beards and ridiculously long hair, who looked as if they had been outfitted in a Haight-Ashbury fire sale; and a scattering of prim, short-haired bureaucrats in short-sleeved white shirts, breast pockets stuffed with ballpoint pens. One wall of the room was lined with glass windows and sliding doors that looked out onto the relatively empty motel parking lot. Behind the speaker's rostrum was a large banner proclaiming BAMBI DIED FOR YOUR SINS.

"And now," the Chairperson said proudly, "the moment you've been waiting for. Our guest speaker certainly needs no introduction . . ."

A rather smug person seated nearby the Chairperson smiled in the grand manner. He was about thirty-five and dressed in an ill-fitting summer suit. He was wearing hi-tech, wire-rimmed glasses. The smug man about to be presented to the Friends of Nature was just now trying to claim the attentions of the person beside him. This was a lovely young lady in high-priced Eddie Bauer *chic,* with long blond hair, blonder than sunlight. Still, with a Nikon slung around her slender neck, she managed to look as if she was ready for a hike up Mount Baldy. Despite all this, Pamela Glover appeared to be slightly, ever-so-faintly . . . *drafty.* And Arthur J. Foyt—our Mr. Smug—was very interested.

Foyt whispered to her as the Chairperson droned on. "This is a terrific turnout for the meeting."

"Oh, yeah, terrific!"

"I suppose you came here to hear me speak."

"Not really," Pamela Glover said. "I'm into trees."

"Trees?" echoed Arthur J. Foyt. The breasts before him were yummy.

"The Friends of Nature love trees. So I come to the meetings."

"Hmmm. That's really interesting." He studied her crossed knees.

"I love anybody who loves trees."

Foyt brightened. "They happen to be a great passion of mine."

"You know what's best about trees?"

Foyt leaned closer. "No, what?"

"The way you can lay under them," Pamela Glover said dreamily, "on a moonlit night, with the leaves rustling in a soft summer wind and—ball your brains out."

The Chairperson moved right along, ". . . he led the campaign to ban the use of electric toothbrushes and to sound the alarm about the possible relationship between library paste and rickets." She paused, importantly. "It is my privilege to present to you the Assistant Administrative Director of the Highway Safety Enforcement Unit of the National Highway Traffic Safety Administration of the United States Department of Transportation . . . Mr. Arthur J. Foyt!"

Foyt stood up, still eyeing Pamela Glover with unmixed emotions, and with pompous nods, received the standing ovation.

He cleared a sheaf of papers from his briefcase and neatly arranged them on the speaker's rostrum. Scanning the audience, he cleared his throat. Pamela Glover looked on, her face serene.

"It's a pleasure to be back here in Darien," Foyt began, "where so many people are engaged in the pitched battle to save our environment. Don't think for a moment that we in Washington don't appreciate your Mother's March to ban the sale of colored toilet paper to help reduce rectal cancer. . . ."

As his words rolled out over the rapt audience, a car could be seen through the windows of the meeting room, rolling up, and parking parallel to the windows. A low, ugly machine painted in gray primer, it was none other than the stock car last seen in the hands of David Pearson and Stan Barrett—they had obviously heeded Uncle Domer's advice. But now the vehicle had stalled and David climbed out to check under the hood. He gestured wildly to Stan to start the engine. All this as Arthur J. Foyt continued his fascinating spiel. The Friends of Nature were enthralled.

". . . a grateful nation extends its thanks. But today I want to direct my remarks to an old and familiar enemy . . ."

Foyt strode to a nearby flip chart positioned to his left, and opened the first page so that all could see. It was a drawing of a large, chrome-encrusted automobile. The audience shuddered.

". . . the American automobile!" roared Arthur J. Foyt.

Upon the words, David Pearson revved the stock car engine in a deafening crescendo to an awful titanic roar. The sonic vibration shattered the motel windows, filling the meeting room with the unbearable sound and clouds of choking exhaust smoke that all sensitive environmentalists' ears and noses and throats could very well do without. The Friends of Nature, seized with shock and anger, rose *en masse* in righteous wrath as Arthur J. Foyt made his way to the broken windows, his face now contorted with fury.

He yelled and gestured with alternating degrees of frenzy, but so intent were David and Stan on tuning their engine that they neither saw him nor heard him. Foyt spotted the Chairperson over and above the din and confusion of the room, and shouted something to her. Then he dashed for the main hallway door.

At that precise moment, less than a block away from Ye Olde English Inne, Mad Dog and Batman coming on hard in their GMC pickup saw nothing but a parking lot now jammed with cars, the traffic remaining on the street heavy as well. Mad Dog showed his teeth. "There's the motel. Looks like the damn place is plugged with cars."

"I can't handle this traffic," Batman, now at the wheel, complained.

"Grab your lunchpail," Mad Dog ordered. "This may get a little weird!"

Batman gunned the engine of the GMC and

cranked the wheel. The heavy truck jumped the curb with a roar and crashed into the parking lot of the motel. Finding a few yards of open pavement, Batman accelerated and pointed his nose straight for the glass-walled front office. Just then, Arthur J. Foyt, striding with irritated briskness, gained the very lobby of Ye Olde English Inne—and saw the GMC coming on like a runaway freight train as Batman floored his gas pedal. Arthur J. Foyt froze in midstride: his Nemesis was targeting in on him dramatically.

All unaware, the desk clerk was lazily registering a pair of incoming guests. As the rumbling roar reached their ears, all three looked up. The monster truck was bearing down on them like King Kong gone amok. The clerk and customers squawked in fright, scattering to the four winds as the GMC lurched into the lobby and struck a large leather couch, bunting it clear across the room as it came on. The couch caught Foyt at the knees and sent him looping over its top.

Finally, the GMC braked to a shuddery stop, swaying as it did so, in the center of the motel lobby.

Mad Dog and Batman looked down from the cab of the truck at the desk clerk who rose trembling from the ruins, much like a bartender after a gunfight in an old Western movie. His rimless glasses were askew, his bow tie crooked now and his lower lip was quivering. The smoke in the lobby settled.

"You running this fleabag?" Mad Dog snarled.

"Ah, uh—uh . . . uh . . . ah . . ." The clerk could not speak at all.

"Where's the goddamn hookers?"

"Ah—aha—what?"

"Hookers, man. Where's the hookers?"

The clerk was still stunned. "We . . . don't have . . . any . . . hookers."

Mad Dog was outraged.

"What'dya mean you don't have no hookers? You ain't trying to tell me you make your money just handing out room keys?"

Arthur J. Foyt, unnoticed and unconscious, lay just out of sight behind the overturned leather couch.

* * *

A shining ambulance, fully decked out with colorful decals, flashing lights and an air of authority, rolled to a stop outside Ye Olde English Inne. The flanks of the vehicle of mercy bore the words: TRANSCONTINTENTAL MEDI-VAC. J. J. McClure and Victor stepped out. Transformed, they were dressed in paramedic uniforms and looked every inch the part. And they arrived as if the dazed clerk had prayed for them. He staggered toward them the way Muslims lurch toward Mecca.

"Thank goodness," the clerk stammered. "We've had a terrible accident." He clutched

J. J. McClure. Victor made a face.

"Hey," J. J. backed off. "We'd like to help but we're off duty, chum." The wreckage in the motel lobby meant nothing to him.

"There's a man in there who looks bad. Maybe he's dead—"

"Then you would probably want to call the coroner."

J. J. and Victor walked across the lobby, picking their way through the rubble. The GMC squatting there with Mad Dog and Batman sitting unconcernedly in the cab brought a smile to J. J.'s face.

He kept the smile as he looked up at the two lobby-destroyers.

"I probably don't have to tell you this but the parking lot is out there." He gestured.

Mad Dog's face was dead-pan for a moment, then he guffawed like a minstrel. "Yeah. I know. Brakes went out. We feel terrible about it."

Victor had finally gone with the clerk to inspect the fallen and prostrate form of Arthur J. Foyt. Victor's eyebrows arched. "Hey, J. J. This guy don't look too good."

J. J. sighed and eased on over. He stared down at Foyt, as though professionally gauging the victim's condition. "I dunno. Just looks like he had his bell rung to me."

The clerk was frantic with all this talk. "Can't you do something? I mean, that's your job!"

J. J. consulted Victor. "What do you think, colleague? I really hate to work on our day off."

62

The clerk was choking now. "Will you guys do something? This man's life is hanging by a thread—"

At that moment, a waiter emerged from the adjacent bar. He was carrying a trayload of drinks. On the tray was a quart bottle of soda water. J. J. winked, snatched the bottle from the tray and capping his thumb over the opening, shook the bottle furiously. With dead aim, tried and true, he bent over Foyt and blasted him with a veritable Niagara.

"This is tricky," J. J. murmured, very professionally, for the clerk's benefit. "The procedure is dangerous, you see. Too much up the nostrils can affect the sinuses."

He triggered one final blast into Arthur J. Foyt's face, and then handed the bottle back to the horrified, speechless clerk.

"That oughta do it. And don't worry about the bill. Give him an enema and call us in the morning."

He winked again and Foyt sputtered like a drowning swimmer, clutched his throat, coughed, hacked and sneezed hard and—came awake. He sat up, blinking like an owl. J. J. and Victor nodded their mutual approval, as if medical science was everything, in the end. Their bedside manner was flawless.

Through the shattered windows came a series of mad noises that had everyone looking. The sound of an approaching car shaped up as a white Rolls Royce trying to navigate the parking lot in a series of crazy, tire-screeching loops, and false starts and stops among the packed vehicles. The young Sheik had arrived on the scene, pledging his all for Islam again. Unfortunately, from his sitting position, Arthur J. Foyt was witness to all this: his Enemy, the Car, once more. It was too much for his demoralized brain and soul. His eyes rolled up into his head, showing the whites, and he flopped back again to his former position on the floor. This time, no one noticed.

J. J., ignoring the wild Rolls Royce, had propelled the clerk toward the registration desk. Victor followed dutifully.

"Now that we've cured the patient, how about getting us our room? By the way, where's the bar? Always have a couple of belts before surgery. Keeps the hand steady, you know."

The clerk, on the verge of collapse himself, could only point feebly in the proper direction. For him, it was shaping up as a day to remember. Or forget.

J. J. McClure paused in passing to give Arthur J. Foyt one final spraying with the soda water.

Arthur J. Foyt was hammered where he lay.

The bar, it seemed, was an upstairs affair, a balcony setup. J. J. and Victor rose to the occasion, so to speak, taking the curving stairway on the dead run.

Out in the parking lot, the Sheik's Rolls Royce made one final lap around the lot and then slid around a corner, out of sight. The two Bedouin tribesmen out there on the sand had been quite correct about the young Sheik not even being able of driving goats around an oasis. He was an angel-maker, First Class.

Yet the Rolls Royce, and the young Sheik, appeared behind the motel and found a home at last. There in a huge lot, Cannonball cars and vehicles, a bevy of wheeled wonders, were filling the setting. People were packing luggage, fiddling with engines, installing driving lights, and generally standing around yammering and laughing. The Rolls Royce managed a full stop in the middle of this gathering of the Cannonball clan, those drivers and codrivers and just plain passengers who all wanted to win the Cannonball Memorial Trophy Dash.

Work on the cars continued. All the systems were being readied for The Big Race. More machinery was arriving. A local Darien police car eased through the crowded lot, cruising slowly, but it did not stop. Music blared somewhere, lending another festive touch to the scene. Everybody seemed to be having a good time. In anything, the preparation, the suspense, the visions of the future, are all—often, planning is more fun than the Trip itself.

A bouncing, rhythmic John Lennon special permeated the air of the lovely day. The crowd in the lot worked in time to the beat, young at heart and happy.

The young Sheik in the white Rolls Royce got into the spirit of things, too. Bounding from his vehicle, he raised the hood and tried to look busy. The Cannonball clan worked on, industriously. Hope was the thing with wheels on.

* * *

The bar that night was filled to overflowing. It had become the Cannonball Lounge, welcoming all drivers, passengers and peripherals into its warm, friendly environs. Ye Olde English Inne was determined to make a mint with the coming sensation, Law or no Law.

Curious locals were there too, to join in the fun, mix with the action and see what was what. The joint was jumping, literally; drinking, conviviality and fun were the order of the day—and night. Eat, drink and be merry was the phrase of the hour, for tomorrow you might win a race!

J. J. McClure and Victor were seated close to the long, packed bar, at a table they had taken because a pair of stunning women were seated nearby. J. J. was planning the first move for Marcie Thatcher and Jill Rivers, the Lamborghini team, though they had not even glanced in his direction. Both females were of the spectacular and gorgeous variety—one blond, one brunette—their designer jeans, tight blouses and filled-out curves put them in the 10 class, all the way.

66

Before J. J. could make his move, Mad Dog materialized and slid a chair to the beauties' table. The women looked at Mad Dog as if he had crawled out from under a rock, but that black worthy was not one to be put down by mere scathing looks.

He grinned wolfishly. "You know, sometimes, you can't lose."

Marcie said, "Huh?"

Jill very coolly murmured, "What's that got to do with us?"

"Tonight," Mad Dog announced, "happens to be one night when I am available."

Marcie Thatcher, intelligent-looking as well as beautiful, raised an eyebrow. She was almost amused. "Yeah? So what?"

"That means I'm yours for the evening—although don't think you're just going to buy me dinner and toss me on the rack."

Marcie Thatcher and Jill Rivers regarded him with that icy stare reserved for dopes, morons, slobs, clods and losers.

Mad Dog hardly noticed. Black was beautiful in his book.

As J. J. and Victor considered an opening ploy, Pamela Glover, tall and cool, with Arthur J. Foyt at her side, entered the bar and crossed the crowded room, heading for the vacant booth adjacent to J. J. and Victor's table. They were carrying on an animated conversation by the looks of it. J. J. caught a glimpse of the long-legged, long-haired, sun-splashed blonde out of the corner of one quick eye. He liked very much what he saw. Ms. Glover saw his engrossing look and immediately catalogued it for future reference.

"Arthur, are you sure you feel well enough to have dinner? We could have bean sprouts sent up to the room."

Foyt bravely shook his head. Nobility shone from his smug face. "I'll be okay. I'd just like to get my hands on those Hell's Angels who were driving that damned truck."

Pamela stiffened. "Those maniacs outside the window. All that awful noise and everything . . ." Cannonballers were not her cup of tea.

"Them too," Foyt agreed. "But it's probably just as well. I'm a wild bull when I lose my temper."

"I just love wild bulls," Pamela Glover trilled.

Arthur J. Foyt's eyes found the faces of J. J. McClure and Victor just then and he halted dead in his tracks before them. He grabbed Pamela's arm, excitedly.

"Holy cow! It's *them!*"

"Them? Who them?"

"Those two phonies who shot me with the soda water." Foyt set his teeth, grimly. "There's going to be trouble."

"Easy, Arthur. They could be part of a terrorist group or something!" They stood stock-still watching J. J. and Victor, who casually returned their attention to the two females and Mad Dog's pitiful courtship. Foyt shook his head, confused.

"I dunno, but the bar is filling up with some real hoodlums. Maybe it's a VFW Convention or something. Those people always raise hell when they get away from home. Either way, I'm going to find out. Come on—" Quickly, he slipped into the booth next to J. J. and Victor, dragging Pamela down with him. He pressed an eager ear to the leather cushion, attempting to eavesdrop, albeit not too cleverly. He was not at all a subtle man.

J. J. and Victor could be heard above the roar of the crowd.

"To pull off this ambulance scam," J. J. was saying, "we need a doctor. You know that, don't you, Victor? And we made a deal that you'd get him."

"I know, I know, but it's not that easy."

"What about your shrink?"

"No way. He's got a horrible phobia about losing his driver's license."

The eye contact with Pamela Glover had been reestablished. J. J. and she were flirting, and with all the preliminaries—to which the busy Arthur J. Foyt was totally oblivious.

"Don't we all, Victor." Turning away from Pamela, J. J. responded to the phobia comment. "So how about your cousin? I thought you said he was a possibility."

"He was, but he already lost his license."

"For speeding?"

"No," Victor sighed. "Malpractice.'

"Goddammit, Victor, I gave you that responsibility! You were going to find a doctor, and now you screwed up! I'm getting damned tired of you screwing up!''

Arthur J. Foyt kept on listening, spellbound.

Victor was beginning to feel great pressure in his brain. And now he was showing it, too. He began to twitch visibly, a vibration coursing through his pudgy body. J. J. threw up his hands in disgust and returned his wandering attention to the two chicks and the absolutely luckless Mad Dog, who had finally been rebuffed. Thoroughly totalled out. He was standing now, groping for an exit line, at least. The girls were practically yawning in his face, particularly Marcie.

"Okay," Mad Dog growled. "This is my last offer. I buy dinner and I throw *you* in the rack."

Marcie killed him dead in his boots. "Look, Slick. Why don't you get back to your Scout Troop before you get in trouble? It's past eleven and I'll bet Mum and Dad don't even know where you are."

Mad Dog smiled sheepishly and slunk off into the crowd in disgrace. J. J., watching all the way and waiting for the opening, leaned over to Victor and motioned toward the girls.

"I wonder if those broads have ever played against varsity competition," he whispered. Then he smiled and, leaning on his elbows, called over to the twin knockouts. "Hi, there! Come down to watch all us Cannonballers, huh?"

Marcie Thatcher eyed him with cool appraisal. It was difficult to know what she thought at that moment.

"Not quite," she said. "We're running the Cannonball. *Very* quickly."

In the next booth, Arthur J. Foyt hissed at Pamela Glover.

"Terrorists, my eye! These people make the PLO look like the Sisters of Charity! These guys are Cannonballers!"

"What's that?" Pamela Glover blinked, brushing at her long blond hair. "A bowling team?"

J. J. was soon into heavy conversation with the fine females now, but their aloofness and lack of interest was discouraging. Still, he pressed his suit, as they say in the old romantic novels—and *not* with a steam iron.

"How about I buy you a drink and we share our race strategies?"

"We'll pass the drink," Marcie answered. "How about fifty gallons of high test?"

"High-test?" J. J. wagged his head. "You wouldn't be Enzo Ferrari in drag, would you?"

"I wouldn't talk." Jill Rivers suddenly zinged him from her side of the table. "You look like the parking attendant from 'General Hospital.' "

Marcie had obviously had enough. "C'mon, Jill. Let's replace that ignition wire and get some sleep." Both sensational ladies rose from the table. J. J. knew when he was licked. He smiled resignedly. You couldn't win them all, even if you liked to.

"I gotta admit you had me fooled. From a distance you come on like *Cosmo* Girls. Up close you act more like the editors of *Motor Trend*. See you around the grease rack."

J. J. McClure turned away, leaving the ladies to whomsoever, only to spy the incredible Victor, who had brought Marcie Thatcher and Jill Rivers to halt on the way out. All were suddenly engaged in an animated tête-à-tête. J. J. McClure shook his head and looked around for Pamela Glover in the next booth.

Which is why he missed seeing Victor stalk off triumphantly with Marcie Thatcher and Jill Rivers in his wake.

Captain Chaos was about to go into action, again.

* * *

Morris Fenderbaum and Jamie Blake were also in that crowded bar. Las Vegas, Nevada, was a long way off—perhaps a lifetime.

Both were attired in cassocks, dark and forbiddingly severe. They both at least had the grace to look uncomfortable in their disguises. Seated on cushioned, jacked-up stools at the long counter, each was coddling his misery with strong drink. In fact, Fenderbaum had ordered a killer, and the bartender, pleased to have such high-class clientele for a change, barely noticed. Still—

"That'll be a *triple* Scotch on the rocks, you say, Father?"

Fenderbaum nodded, miserable, and Blake rushed to his defense.

"He's had a hard day, my son. The whole American Nazi Party came in for a confession." Feisty Fenderbaum grimaced as the bartender padded off to mix the drink. Neither Blake nor Fenderbaum noticed the rather meek-looking traveling salesman seated on the next stool. Not that it mattered. The gambler and his driver were tired.

"That sonofabitch oughta mind his own business. I've got a mind to smack him right in the mouth."

The traveling salesman looked up from his own drink, shocked.

Jamie Blake did not help much, either.

"This damned collar is about to choke me. We should have been Methodists."

The salesman gurgled into his drink, spitting, choking.

A few moments later, Fenderbaum had warmed himself with some heavy Scotch. He surveyed the room at large, his slight, wiry form pugnacious at the bar. Blake was dreamily staring into his own glass, more tiredly handsome than ever and thinking about the race.

"Lookit these stiffs," Fenderbaum rasped. "We got this thing won, hands down. I may call the Greek and put another ten grand on this caper.''

Jamie Blake nodded. ''I'll buy that. It's your dough.''

The traveling salesman now began to wobble in disbelief.

Across the crowded floor, in the booth where Pamela Glover sat in all her blond loveliness, J. J. McClure had begun his opening round. With pure and masculine finesse he grinned.

''Hi! Want to fool around?''

Pamela sniffed the air. ''You're one of those weirdo volleyballers.''

''You mean Cannonballers. But I ain't one of them.''

''Oh, yeah.'' Skepticism dominated her voice. ''What are you dressed up like that for?''

''Humanitarian reasons. I'm a millionaire philanthropist—I just travel around the world in my ambulance, helping people. Find a flood or tornado and I'll be there. I catch *all* the big-name hurricanes.''

Pamela Glover was now hooked. And no longer suspicious. He had said the magic words. He had talked *environment* and *caring*. ''That really sounds like a beautiful thing.''

J. J. smelled pay dirt. He moved closer.

''Yeah.'' He managed to sound reflective. ''You gotta do what you can. After all, God didn't put us here to hurt each other, did he?''

''That's beautiful. You must be a very sensitive person. I'll bet you're a fan of Rod McKuen's. Me, I'm into trees. Have you ever heard of Joyce Kilmer?"

"Sure," J. J. said.

"She wrote a really terrific poem about a tree," Pamela said.

"He."

"Huh?"

"He. Joyce Kilmer was a man, Beauty."

"Wow, that's far out. Still, it's a terrific poem."

"Yeah, I know. It made all the papers."

J. J. detected a yo-yo somewhere in his new-found lady love. Still, she was an eyeful. And those white teeth—

"You know what I like best about trees?" Pamela kept on coming.

"The sap."

"What I like best about trees," Pamela Glover repeated her theme song, "is the way you can lay under them and—"

A waiter walking by, with a giant teetering tray of glasses, heard it all. The results were disastrous. Waiter and tray hit the floor almost together, with a crashing symphony of tinkling glass. J. J., however, had already caught sight of something far more interesting. *"Good God!"* he roared. *"He's done it again!"*

Victor had reappeared in the crowded bar, a triumphant Victor. A no-longer-trembling Victor. A victorious Victor, who was just replacing his Captain Chaos mask in his belt pouch, and folding his crazy cape. To either side of him were Marcie Thatcher and Jill Rivers. The girls were radiant, gorgeous, smiling

75

and—disheveled. In truth, both looked thoroughly taken care of—into the realms of Cloud Nine and Seventh Heaven, as it were.

Both Tens drifted off to their rooms, leaving the pudgy superman as if they were walking on air. The bar buzzed with approval. Everyone had seen those affectionate kisses bestowed on Victor, on each cheek, by the departing women.

Fathers Blake and Fenderbaum had missed none of it, either.

Blake snarled: "Look at those chicks! . . . If we had been Methodists, we'd have a helluva shot at getting laid."

"You got that right." Father Fenderbaum belched.

The traveling salesman's eyes searched ceiling-ward as he crossed himself, rapidly and violently.

Victor trooped to the table where J. J. and Pamela Glover sat in mutual conclave. J. J. gave Pamela one long look and then regarded Victor with mingled respect and supplication.

"Victor, how about loaning me that mask for about an hour?"

"Oh, I couldn't do that. You know it's *his* mask . . ."

"You can't blame me for trying."

J. J. gestured to Pamela and she continued her song.

". . . like I was saying, what I really like about trees is the way you can lay under them and . . ."

"I've got good news," Victor interjected,

brightly.

"Later, Victor," J. J. demurred, eyeing Pamela. "Later . . ."

"Yeah, but I think I've got a way to get a doctor . . ."

"That's terrific. Let's talk about it, later."

"But we need a doctor—"

"I know we need a doctor!" J. J.'s voice rose in irritation. "But right now I've got some other things to attend to. Get it? Now get lost!"

Victor looked crestfallen, but Pamela Glover barely noticed the sometime masked man. She was still into her dream-world of trees . . .

* * *

Meanwhile, upstairs in one of Ye Olde English Inne's happily harmonious suites, two gentlemen were in very earnest conversation. Indeed, they were old friends and their reunion might have been a touching one, were it not so businesslike.

Shakey Finch, the Pizza King, former world champion cross-country motorcyclist, had entered the suite of Bradford W. Compton, to find that mad motorcycle jumper, yet very sane Big Businessman, standing back and admiring a glistening Suzuki touring bike that held the center of the room. Compton was exquisitely dressed, as usual. Finch, not much of a clothes horse, was pure working-class. He had always resembled a Dead End kid.

"Hey, Brad, ol' boy—" Shakey squeaked out loud.

"Kindly move out of the doorway, will you?" Compton had left the room door wide open. "You're blocking the light. By the way, who are you?"

"It's me, Shakey," came the puzzled reply.

Bradford W. Compton stared. "Shakey? My God, it is!" His eyes swept over the deepening fat on the man in the doorway. "But—but—the last time I saw you, you were—how shall I say it?—*svelte?*"

"What can I tell you?" Shakey sighed. "In the pizza business when things get slow, you eat the inventory."

Bradford W. Compton looked worried at that.

"Listen, old man, that may be all well and good in the pizza business, but extra weight just won't work in the Cannonball. I mean, you don't need a motorcycle. You need the Super Chief."

"Extra tonnage or not," Shakey Finch averred, "I'm still the best there is." He pointed to the Suzuki. "I'll ride the wheels off that thing."

"That," Compton sighed, "is what worries me."

"Anything I break, I fix."

Bradford W. Compton shrugged and mounted the Suzuki tourer, squeezing the clutch. "Listen, take a quick look at the adjustment on this, will you? The way it is, with all this weight, we'll burn it out before we hit the George Washington Bridge.''

Shakey Finch nodded, took a couple of wrenches from a tool box and bent to the engine and its problem. Grunting, he made a few precise adjustments. When he came back up for air, he was breathing heavily. But his eyes were twinkling.

"She's perfect now, Brad. Give her a try."

Brad did. All too well.

He hit the starter button and the bike, obviously already in direct drive, went totally out of control, blasting off the floor and right through the room doorway. And careened down the hallway in a burst of forward speed. As Shakey looked on in horror, Bradford W. Compton executed a series of hairbreadth misses, involving walls and furniture.

Compton raced on through the motel proper. First he hit the kitchen, where he bowling-balled a waiter directly out of his flying path, and then he slalomed through the dining room, without touching a thing.

The Suzuki hit the barroom like a released rocket, tearing, zipping, scooting. Compton was handling the machine like a daredevil, perhaps all too unwillingly. J. J. McClure, still busy with Pamela Glover, gave him the idlest of glances as he bulleted by. Pamela Glover jumped.

"Wow, what was that?"

"I think that was the entry from the National Safety Council," J. J. said mockingly. "They're big supporters of Cannonball, you know. Right behind us, all the way.''

Bradford W. Compton kept on going, rocketing through the motel in a mechanical din. Nobody was really safe—including Arthur J. Foyt. That spoilsport ensconced in a nearby room, babbling crazily into the phone.

"Boss, this is the biggest coup in the history of the Safety Enforcement Unit. We blow this Cannonball wide open and then we hit Congress with a budget that'll let us play some real hardball. This is our own Three Mile Island and Love Canal combined!''

Alas, poor Arthur J. Foyt.

The millionaire on the runaway motorcycle blasted through the room door and hit the dresser where the phone was sitting, flinging chunks of furniture in all directions. And also pitching Foyt onto his bed like a flung rag doll. Compton continued on out the window by way of the floor-to-ceiling window and was gone with a bursting crash. Foyt lay stunned on the bed, holding onto the phone in his hand, its severed wires dangling. He shook himself. The bad dream was going on and on, the one that had all begun that day with the Chairperson introducing him gaily to the Friends of Nature. Where had he gone wrong?

A small overhead chandelier, with a last brave shudder, crashed to the floor. The bed in the room began to vibrate gently as its *Magic Fingers* system went to work.

Arthur J. Foyt began to cry like an overgrown child. Even for a would-be humanitarian, this was all just too much. The morning could not come fast enough for Arthur J. Foyt.

Then, still snuffling, he squared his shoulders. He knew what had to be done, and by thunder, he would do it!

FOLLOW THE
CANNONBALL ROAD

The sun had come up over Darien, Connecticut, a flaming round ball of heat and brilliance, bathing the cheery landscape with golden hues. And nowhere was the grand face of Old Sol brighter than above the parking lot of the Lock, Stock and Barrel Restaurant. The setting was all Cannonball, all excitement and preparation and industry.

Crews were loading up their disparate vehicles for the big race. People were tossing luggage into trunks, making adjustments on driving lights, checking their CB radios and radar detectors. Many of the cars were the very same that had surrounded Ye Olde English Inne only the night before. But now, a score or more new ones had been added, accompanied by a lot of new faces—some stranger than ever.

A middle-aged couple picking their way among the crowds of mismatched vehicles, shook their heads at all the activity. The man wore a blue blazer and a red tie, the woman was stylishly dressed in a beige pants suit. Both were typical, upper-middle-class Fairfield County

WASPs, for whom joy, free spirits and the full life can be a bit unnerving at times. The woman was amazed.

"My God, Norman, why didn't you tell me all this was going on? Why, we could have had a cocktail party!"

Her husband winced, noticeably.

Meanwhile, back in the sad rubble of his room at the motel, Arthur J. Foyt was going into action. He had had enough and it was time to move—forcibly. Still in his pajamas, Foyt was on the phone, getting matters underway. The curtains were blowing gently into the void of broken glass left by the misadventures of Bradford W. Compton, the bed was still tilted at a discreet angle, *Magic Fingers* whirring away. From this Waterloo, Arthur J. Foyt was determined to wrest Victory. No Napoleon jazz for him!

"—Operator, get me the Darien police. This is an emergency!"

Soon, at the other end of the line, a heavy-faced police sergeant, sipping a cup of coffee and fiddling with a note pad on a cluttered desk, dutifully listened to all Arthur J. Foyt had to complain about. The sergeant shared Mr. Foyt's outrage.

"Yeah, Mr. Foyt, we got it handled. Those are some of the same bums who busted down the motel lobby. Believe me, they won't dare to so much as squeal a tire in Darien or my boys'll be all over them like a cheap suit. You can count on that!"

But Arthur J. Foyt was only slightly mollified by that and continued to rave from his end of the line. He sounded apoplectic.

The sergeant continued to listen, scratching away on his note pad. Gilbert and Sullivan had summed it up—a policeman's lot was never a very happy one. And not the least of the trouble was civilians like Arthur J. Foyt. Still, Foyt had a case; the sergeant had no love for Cannonballers either.

It was going to make for a helluva lousy, sweet police day!

Back at the Lock, Stock and Barrel, amidst the furor and the excitement, a steel-gray Aston-Martin DB-6 glided into view. At the wheel was Seymour Goldfarb, as natty as ever, super-cool and every inch Roger Moore's look-alike. At his side was the sort of stunning brunette you might see in a James Bond movie. The impeccable Seymour parked expertly near a cardtable that had been set up in the shelter of the restaurant. His keen eyes appraised the scene, looking for possible points of ambush and retreat. There was a young girl at the table, on duty.

Goldfarb smiled engagingly as he approached the girl on silent, springy feet. "Good day. I'm here to participate in your little jaunt to California." His clipped, purring British accent was lost on the girl who examined his card very carefully.

"Of course. If you'll sign here . . ."

"Obviously, you do not recognize me, my dear."

"No," the girl admitted, blankly. "Should I?"

"Were you a patron of the better-class films, you would."

"Such as?"

"Oh—*Boldthumb, From Russia With Shove, Thundernut*—"

Seymour Goldfarb extracted an expensive pen from the folds of his dapper suit and smoothly set down on the proferred list his name.

'Roger Moore' he wrote in a fine, script hand.

A teenage boy ambling by spotted him and quickly raised an Instamatic camera to snap Seymour Goldfarb's handsome face.

Unperturbed, the man with a mission reached into the breast pocket of his tuxedo suit and drew forth a pair of sunglases. He smiled winningly at the girl who was signing entrants in.

"I realize the novelty of a major celebrity entering your little race, but please resist the temptation and keep the media coverage to a minimum. There's a good girl."

Again, the girl was blank-faced as Seymour Goldfarb made his exit.

She looked at the signature on the paper, shrugged and without further reaction tossed it on the pile collecting on her card table.

* * *

The Organizer of the Cannonball Memorial Trophy Dash, from sea to shining sea, had mounted a large garbage barrel in front of the Lock, Stock and Barrel Restaurant. From this vantage point, he could look out and see some several hundred crewmen, curious bystanders and the same old rubberneckers who collected for any public gathering. The Organizer reveled in the sunlight as he delivered his announcements and rules of the game—that is to say, the race.

The sun blazed down. The lot was as quiet as a church. This was a big moment for all Cannonballers everywhere.

"Welcome," the Organizer boomed, "to the motorized version of the Bay of Pigs. I feel like Lord Raglan addressing the Light Brigade just before the Charge. As near as we can figure, every highway patrol this side of Manila is out there waiting. What's more, Interstate Eighty in Pennsylvania has so many potholes it looks like a tank trap, and it's threatening to snow in the Rockies. Otherwise, the Cannonball ought to be a stroll in the park. . . ."

His audience burst into laughs, roars and cheers of alternating decibels, punctuated by clapping of hands.

Behind the crowd, several vehicles were conspicuous by dint of their uniqueness and type: the black Lamborghini, the squat brown GMC pickup truck, the white Rolls Royce, Seymour Goldfarb's Aston-Martin DB-6, the white ambulance—in fact, Victor had just slid the ambulance to a stop and J. J. McClure was hurrying to him, anxiously.

"Okay," the Organizer carried on. "I guess you all know the rules, if you can call them that. You can take any route between the Lock, Stock and Barrel and the Portofino Inn in Redondo Beach. You punch out on the time clock here and punch in there. The team with the least elapsed time is the winner. It's that simple." He paused, meaningfully. "The present record is held by David Heinz and David Yarborough at thirty-two hours fifty-one minutes."

Victor had gone around the ambulance to its rear, as a shimmering red Ferrari also moved further into the parking lot. Behind the wheel sat a gloomy 'Father' Blake, while 'Father' Fenderbaum rode the passenger seat. J. J. closed in on Victor as the Organizer closed up shop.

". . . now one last thing. A tradition with the Cannonball is the first car to start—on the 'pole' position as it were—will be those famed international *raconteurs* and scofflaws, the Polish Racing Drivers of America!"

The crowd now went wild as a funk rock band buried somewhere behind them struck up the Cannonball theme, a wild, romping score designed to make everyone feel like they could win a race, any race. As the music thumped and whomped, the crowd thinned, breaking up into small, enthusiastic groups, making ready for the

87

jump-off. Or rather, the punching in—on the time clocks, the most important piece of business for all competitors. But the first card had to be the PRDA card—The Polish Racing Drivers of America. The countdown from Five to One began. The card was yanked and one of the PRDA, sprinted toward his idling van just outside the Lock, Stock and Barrel. As he sprang aboard, the crowd roared. Strong cheers sounded all around.

The van accelerated down the alley of people, parting them, and then was gone. The first car had started. The Cannonball was on!

For real. For sure. The PRDA had got the whole thing going. The funky rock band poured it on, then, louder than ever.

If such a thing was possible.

* * *

J. J. McClure had cornered Victor as the Polish van disappeared from view amidst the cheers of the crowd. Victor looked very unhappy.

J. J. groaned aloud.

"No doctor? Still no doctor, Victor?"

"I got everything else," Victor whined.

"No goddamn doctor!"

"Sixty gallons of gas. The auxiliary tank is full."

"Doctor, Victor. No doctor!"

"The CB and the radar detector are all checked out—"

J. J. refused to be pacified by all this efficiency.

"Goddammit, Victor, it's your responsibility to get us a doctor." He checked his watch, wincing. "We've got twenty-four minutes before we start this race. Last night you said you had a line on a doctor. And I want him! I don't care if it's Doctor Livingston, Doctor Zhivago or Doctor Kildare, or if you find him in a hospital, nut house or country club bar, I want a *doctor!*"

The unhappy Victor clambered aboard the ambulance and drove away again as J. J. fumed where he stood. In the red Ferrari, the bogus priests had watched it all. Morris Fenderbaum, jaw jutting, pointing a finger warningly.

"See that tall one? J. J. McClure. We gotta watch him. He's almost won this thing a couple of times."

Jamie Blake snorted. "So what? That little blimp is the one. He puts his mask on and he'll suck your hub caps off!"

The battered blue Berlinetta Ferrari now roared away from the starting line. The crowd continued to cheer. Anything in motion now would draw a response. Father Blake, edgy and impatient, had drifted from his own Ferrari over to Marcie Thatcher, who was about to climb into the bullet-nosed black Lamborghini. Her hips were a public scandal. Jamie Blake had pulled his coat collar up, trying to conceal his priest's outfit. How can you make time with a chick if she thinks you're a Holy Joe?

"Hi. Nice-looking piece you've got here." He indicated the black car. "Cunningly disguised as a racing car. Clever. The cops will never give you a second glance."

"At two hundred and twenty miles an hour, they won't get a second glance." Blake considered that and nodded, smiling.

"When we get to California maybe we oughta have dinner. I know a little place in Palos Verdes . . ."

Marcie Thatcher, eyebrows arched, saw that Blake, comfortable and in full swing, had unknowingly released his hands from his coat collar and plunged them into his pockets. The priest outfit fairly screamed to be recognized. Marcie smiled maliciously.

"Wait a minute, Father. That's a no-no. Haven't you heard? It's been a rule for nearly two thousand years."

"Er—" Jamie Blake tried to recover. "I come from the liberal wing of the Church."

"Oh, yeah? Well, I'm an Irish-Catholic and I don't think the Spanish Inquisition stopped soon enough!" She ran her eyes over Blake with pure malice. "Keep the faith, *Father.*"

With that parting nasty, she slid behind the wheel of the Lamborghini, fired the engine, jammed the car into gear and shot from the parking lot with a roar, spraying Jamie Blake with flying stones as she left. Morris Fenderbaum came up at that moment, looking curious.

"Well," he snapped. "You set us up for California or what?"

Jamie Blake, fuming, angrily whirled on the little man, grabbed him by the lapels and barked:

"Next time—*Methodists!*"

Never ever in his life had Jamie Blake so thoroughly despised holier-than-thou chicks like Marcie Thatcher, nice ass or no nice ass!

Behind the bogus, grumbling Fathers, the crowd roared anew as the time clock digested another card—another hopeful, more wheels.

Another Cannonball entry hit the road.

The race was warming up in earnest, now.

From sea to shining sea. With everybody having a gimmick and a disguise of some kind to foil that Law, which would surely try to block them. You could not win the Cannonball going fifty-five miles an hour.

* * *

Two men dressed in high-fashioned Hollywood clothes, with the requisite dark sunglasses, modified Afros, dangling gold chains and an air of life in continual sunlight, stood beside their Excalibur, clocking the rolling entrants as they punched in and took off on the road to the Portofino Inn in Redondo Beach, California.

Both were extremely confident. One, named Shelly, spoke for them both, now. "How does it feel, Manny boy, to know you have this thing in the bag before we even start?"

Manny nodded at that. His smile was as wide as Australia.

"Yeah, baby. I'm tired of standing around here with these stiffs. Let's boogie back to the bar and have a couple of hits before we start."

Easy, relaxed and certain were Shelly and Manny. The Cannonball, as Shelly had said, was in the bag. The bar of the Lock, Stock and Barrel was an oasis in Jerksville, as far as they were concerned—Nowhere, U.S.A. But liquor is liquor. No matter where you find it.

Yet, none of the other entrants felt the same as Shelly and Manny did. Everybody else was taking it quite seriously. For example—

The young Sheik, settled on the back seat of his resplendently white Rolls Royce, was getting ready. His ticker-tape machine that kept him on top of Wall Street and the world money news was in position. His bodyguards were trying to relax, trying not to think about the future.

The Subaru racing team—the two Japanese drivers—had wound their white *kamikaze* scarves around their foreheads, prepared to do-or-die for the good of their company. They toasted each other with little paper cups of ceremonial *sake* and murmured to each other the sacred oaths. Nippon tradition must not be put aside, not even for the Cannonball!

Fathers Morris Fenderbaum and Jamie Blake adjusted each other's collars, solemnly vowing to win this one, with or without the help of the Good Lord. Blake, veteran of the Grand Prix and Indianapolis Speedway races, was seriously considering prayer as a means to the end. Fenderbaum, wiry and pugnacious, was banking only on the Ferrari and Jamie Blake. God had never helped *him* on a roll of the dice.

Bradford W. Compton was fiddling around with a JUST MARRIED sign, draping it over the back of his motorcycle. He was more businesslike than ever. Shakey Finch was desperately trying to fit a blond wig under his crash helmet. He looked more like an overgrown Dead End kid than usual. And he never looked less like a Pizza King or a former champion cross-country motorcyclist.

David Pearson and Stan Barrett were groping under the hood of their ugly gray stock car, as if searching for the one thing that would help them both win the Cannonball—a fine-running engine!

And J. J. McClure was standing alone in the crowd, mournful and exasperated, watching as one Cannonball team after another left the starting gate. Worry was not the word. He looked at his watch ten times in ten minutes. The crowd roared anew.

When Victor and the ambulance made a sudden reappearance, he jumped like a jack-in-the-box. Elbowing through the crowd, he ran to meet Victor coming down from the wheel. The

93

rotund mechanic looked as pleased as if his pet gerbils had gotten over their treadmill fetish. His pudgy face was wreathed in a Halloween smile.

"How'd you do?" J. J. bellowed.

"I did it! I got a doctor!"

"Terrific!"

"I gotta warn you." Victor now sounded dangerously apologetic. "You can't expect too much on such short notice."

J. J. frowned, then went to the rear door of the ambulance and whipped it open. The figure revealed thusly was tall, lean, rather contorted, and only the coat of a doctor—albeit stained and dingy white—was proof of that calling. The man's face was gaunt, devilish; a sick smile drooped at a skewed angle from eyes that seemed to look off in opposite directions. J. J. was appalled. This seedy, spavined wreck could not be a medical man, no way. Unless—

"Jesus," he snapped at Victor, "I thought Dr. Frankenstein was dead."

"Doc, this is J. J. McClure." Victor made the peace quickly. "He's gonna make this little trip with us."

"I am honored, sir." A skeletal hand was extended to J. J. "Allow me to introduce myself. I am Doctor Nicholas Van Helsing, practitioner of proctology and other related disciplines; graduate of the University of Rangoon and assorted night classes at the Knoxville, Tennessee College of Faith Healing."

J. J. shook the proffered hand. He was whipped. No, he was *desperate*. "You may be overqualified but we'll take you. You bring your equipment?''

"I never go anywhere without it." Dr. Van Helsing indicated a small black bag on the floor of the ambulance. "However, in my particular line of work, I seldom need anymore than this . . ." His long, crooked middle finger poked out. It was covered with a prophylactic rubber. "—or this—" he continued. The grubby coat parted and coming forth now was a long hypodermic with a very bent, very rusty needle.

J. J. looked at Victor and murmured: "We're going to have to talk about this later."

Dr. Nicholas Van Helsing assumed a professional air.

"And now, sir, before we commence this odyssey, which I understand will carry across this grand nation from sea to shining sea, there is the matter of my compensation. I have determined that my services will require the payment of two thousand dollars."

J. J. McClure stared him down, grinning from ear to ear. "I was thinking more in the neighborhood of two hundred bucks."

Dr. Van Helsing beamed a noble smile. "Fortunately for you, sir, my practice permits me a certain flexibility in price. After reviewing my calendar, I have determined that I have the time to make the trip with you. As for the money—I'll take it."

"Gee," J. J. McClure said. "This is our lucky day."

95

Not far from the starting line, about a thousand yards from the Lock, Stock and Barrel Restaurant, a clapped-out, aged Volvo was camouflaged in a stand of tall trees. Arthur J. Foyt was busy again. This time, he focused a pair of powerful binoculars on the roadway leading from the restaurant. He had seen much that had made him wince and shudder. Still, he was doing his duty as a solid, forthright U.S. Citizen. He had scanned the horizon and had not gone unrewarded. Beside him, as cool and indolent as ever, was Pamela Glover.

"There goes another one. . . ." Foyt cackled diabolically. He strained through the binoculars. "The license number is . . . Nevada, Whiskey—Zebra—Alpha, niner—fiver—zero—Got that?"

Pamela blinked. "Huh?"

Arthur J. Foyt groaned. Why was it so hard for brains to go with beauty? "Just write," he commanded wearily. "WZA—nine—five—oh . . .'

Pamela Glover stuck her tongue between her teeth and scribbled on the steno pad Arthur J. Foyt had provided for the assignment. How did you spell *O?*

At the starting line, Mad Dog and Batman were drawing close to the jump-off point in their brown GMC pickup truck. Mad Dog was at the wheel. Batman had his boots up on the dash, again.

"You gonna use that shortcut to the Inter-state?" he dryly asked his black partner. Mad

J.J. McClure (BURT REYNOLDS) has only one goal: winning the Cannonball Run.

J.J. McClure and his sidekick, Victor (DOM DeLUISE), who often dons mask and cape to become the fearless "Captain Chaos."

As cars and trucks assemble at the starting point of the Cannonball run, parking becomes a real problem.

Stock car racers played by TERRY BRADSHAW and MEL TILLIS devise a new way to wash their car before starting off on the Cannonball Run.

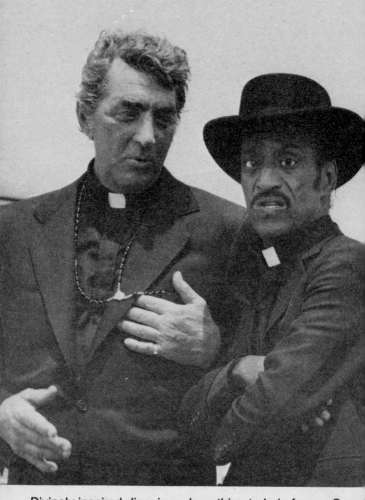

Divinely inspired disguises do nothing to help former Grand
Prix driver Jamie Blake (DEAN MARTIN) and gambler Fen-
derbaum (SAMMY DAVIS, JR.) as they team up to race in the
Cannonball Run.

Fenderbaum, a gambler who will bet on anything he drives in the Cannonball run, here disguised as a priest to fool the cops.

Seymour Goldfarb, Jr. (ROGER MOORE) is a man who thinks he's Moore playing James Bond. Here he kids with his elderly Jewish mother (MOLLY PICON).

Stopping for a six-pack via plane on Main Street, U.S.A. is only one of the many spectacular stunts in THE CANNON-BALL RUN.

Subaru Driver #1 (JACKIE CHAN) drives a futuristic Subaru with a built-in computer.

Victor as Captain Chaos, superhero of his own psyche.

Sheik (JAMIE FARR) is a wealthy oil sheik who drives a white Rolls-Royce as his entry in the Cannonball Run.

The Sheik's sister (BIANCA JAGGER). She doesn't approve of her brother's antics.

Bradford Compton (BERT CONVY) is a Wall Street tycoon who goes for broke when he gets on a motorcycle to compete in the Cannonball Run.

With Bond-like style, Seymour Goldfarb, Jr. makes a hasty exit from his car when he presses the wrong button on his dashboard.

Dr. Nicholas Van Helsing (JACK ELAM) is an unsavory practitioner of proctology and other related disciplines who is recruited to join the ambulance team and lend it an air of nea authenticity.

ERRY BRADSHAW plays a racer driving a red-hot stock car.

MEL TILLIS teams up with Terry to race their stock car in th
Cannonball Run.

Marcie Thatcher (ADRIENNE BARBEAU) is a beautiful daredevil who drives a Lamborghini.

This Oklahoma highway Patrolwoman (VALERIE PERRINE) is the shapeliest Oklahoma State Trooper in history, handing out smiles with speeding tickets.

Jamie Blake finds there's nothing sacred about his disguise when he gets into a free-for-all with a tough motorcycle gang.

Bradford Compton and rider Shakey Finch (WARREN BERLINGER) prove to be real heavyweights in the cycle world as they fight to keep their wheels down, racing across the country in the Cannonball Run.

Dog barked like his namesake.

"Hell, yes. That's what we're here for, ain't it? If you're gonna be a bear, be a grizzly."

Crowd noises had, if anything, increased.

Batman sprang from the truck, ran to the time clock, punched the card in and then leaped back aboard. Mad Dog chortled, gave the truck the gun and blasted away from the starting line with a rush. The crowd thundered its approval. The Cannonball was mounting in thrills and excitement. One team after another, one crazy kind of vehicle after another thundered out of the restaurant parking lot. There was no end to the variety of challengers.

When Mad Dog veered off the roadway farther on, bulldozing through a line of small trees to shortcut his way to the Interstate, it was under the full binocular inspection of an outraged Arthur J. Foyt. The sight of Mother Nature being raped was too much for him. He felt as if he was going to be sick.

"My God, Pamela, did you see that! Those maniacs drove right through those helpless little trees!"

Ms. Glover whimpered in empathy. "That's awful, hurting those little bitty pine trees—" Her eyes went moist, a far-away look transforming their blue depths. "I really love trees. You know why I love trees? Because you can lay under them on a moonlit night . . ."

Foyt was not listening. He was lost in a sea of fury and righteous indignation.

"We're going to get down there and bring this

thing to a screeching halt—right now!" He bent down to start the Volvo engine and grabbed for his shoulder harness. "Buckle up. We're going into action!"

The engine turned over but Foyt was having his troubles with the gearbox. A loud, protesting crunch of gears rose up as Foyt tried to engage the transmission.

Pamela Glover, still misty-eyed, was shivering with secret ecstasy.

Trapped in a car that wouldn't start—Saver-of-the-World *Extraordinaire,* Tree-Lover and Long-Haired Beauty—two intruders, and *not* well-wishers for the Cannonball. How could they be? They knew absolutely nothing about cars or engines. Much less people.

* * *

The white ambulance was now also on the road, hoping for victory and success. J. J. McClure was bent to the wheel, Victor at his side. Dr. Nicholas Van Helsing rode a small jump seat in the rear. J. J. was driving hard. The ambulance shot along the roadway. The hot ball of a sun seemed to follow.

"Okay, guys, here we go. Three thousand madcap, carefree miles . . ." J. J. was in a good mood, no matter what. Driving was a drug to him.

Dr. Nicholas Van Helsing began to sing. Cats in an alley could sound better, but the spirit was right. *"California, here we come . . . right back where . . . we . . ."*

J. J. jerked his head in Victor's direction, heedless of the musical mutilation going on behind him.

"The perfect plan. With imperfect people. First that chick of yours backs out. . . ."

"Because of her bladder," Victor said, defensively. "She just didn't think she could go the distance. You know how that is. . . ."

"Aw, bullshit! Victor, you know it's because she's got some idiot hangup about using public johns."

"Well, gee, J. J.—"

"And now we've got us a doctor straight out of Madame Tussaud's Wax Museum. I feel like I'm running this thing with my fly open."

"If worse comes to worst," Victor suggested, "I can climb into the stretcher back there and act sick."

"That'll do you perfectly," J. J. said grumpily, as much as he hated to snap at Victor. "We'll just tell people you're crazy."

Victor's face assumed an expression of alarm. His round eyes were frightened. "Easy, J. J. *He* never likes to hear me insulted. You know that."

Under his breath, J. J. cursed. Captain Chaos again. Maybe Victor *was* crazy. Who else had an alter ego with a mask and a special uniform, and a double-whammy of some kind?

J. J. McClure stopped talking and paid grim

attention to the wheel and the road. The ambulance was flying along now.

Hell, the Cannonball came first, didn't it? It was the Here and Now, the End-all and the Be-all, for J. J. McClure. It was the chance of a lifetime.

Seymour Goldfarb with his stunning brunette and his silver beauty of an Aston-Martin DB-6 were already well into the race. The sleek, handsome millionaire was having the time of his double life. The brunette was all ears as he regaled her with tales of his past life. Goldfarb had not a single thought about his poor mother back there in the old family mansion in Beverly Hills. What did mother know, anyway?

The Aston-Martin, the vehicle that had so astounded and amused Auric Goldfinger, zipped along the road, eating up the miles.

Hurry, hurry up.

Open up that Golden Gate.

California, here they come . . . for all they're worth. And all they could get out of it. From sea to shining sea for all the marbles.

ALL SYSTEMS GO

Arthur J. Foyt and Pamela Glover had come a cropper, somehow. This was very apparent when J. J. McClure, running hard with his ambulance, reached an intersection and saw the collision. The aging Volvo had met head on with another vehicle of indeterminate make and design. And there was the long-legged, taffy-haired, dizzy blond semaphoring wildly for help. J. J. slowed the ambulance. The big side door slid open as Dr. Nicholas Van Helsing poised at the ready. Pamela exclaimed at sight of the white clothes and the familiar faces of J. J. and Victor.

"Hey, guys. Arthur bumped his head. Could you drop him off at the hospital?"

J. J. grinned his handsome grin. Beauty was a real looker. "Hey, baby, that's what we're here for. Step on board."

Arthur was staggering up to the door, holding his head, clothes askew, keen mind reeling. He looked thoroughly beaten. Pamela Glover clambered into the ambulance without looking at him or lending a hand.

"Go around to the back door," J. J. instructed Arthur J. Foyt. "That's the emergency exit."

Bewildered, Foyt wandered to the rear as Pamela settled inside. As Foyt reached for the back-door handle, J. J. accelerated, and the ambulance charged off once more. Arthur J. Foyt spilled down to the pavement, abandoned, up-ended and forgotten. Pamela Glover was oblivious to his absence as she chattered gaily with J. J. and Victor. Dr. Van Helsing was eyeing her as if he wished she needed a proctologist.

"Boy it's really terrific the way you guys just cruise around helping people," Pamela gushed.

"One of these years it will get us a Nobel Prize," J. J. agreed, eyes on the road. "That's where the bucks are."

Pamela suddenly woke up. She touched J. J.'s shoulder timidly.

"Er . . . excuse me, J. J. I think we forgot Arthur."

"Well, we got you—that's batting five hundred. Nobody's perfect, are they?"

"Maybe we should turn around and get him."

"Nothing we'd rather do. Problem is, we're kind of on a tight schedule. Gotta be in California. That place is *overflowing* with sick people." He shook his head sadly, then snapped his fingers—"Say! Maybe we can pick him up on the way back."

Pamela turned to Victor for an appeal.

"Maybe you could help?"

Victor shook his head. "Naw. I can't do anything—'' Brightening, he reached for his pouch. ''But *he* can!'' He started to rummage for his cape, cowled mask—and that other personality, *Captain Chaos*.

Pamela stared at him in puzzlement. She frowned and whirled on Dr. Van Helsing whose back was to her, now.

''Doctor, can you help me get Arthur?''

The good doctor turned, displaying his hypo with the long rusty needle. He grinned wolfishly. On seeing all this, in a flash, Pamela Glover screamed, and fainted.

''A perfect specimen, gentlemen. May I suggest that I begin my examination immediately?'' A crazed gleam in his wall-eye belied his education. J. J. McClure looked heavenward for help. None was coming.

What *did* come was a flurry of traffic up ahead, a knot of cars, a wolf pack, and he paid attention to the road. Nothing bad ever happened to dizzy blondes. He kept on driving, weaving expertly through the maze of four-wheeled Sunday drivers. He knew what he was doing—trying to win the Cannonball, that's what, and what was more, freaks like Dr. Nicholas Van Helsing weren't going to stop him.

Or fat mechanics who imagined they were someone else. It never rains but it pours. Victor's Captain Chaos—

A blasting car horn up ahead made him get back to proper thinking.

The race *was* to the swift, okay. *Okay*. He would be swift. The ambulance rocketed forward at tremendous speed.

Dr. Nicholas Van Helsing was singing again, murdering the same song as he leered down at the unconscious Pamela Glover.

The miles eroded away, vanishing under the wheels of the big white ambulance. J. J. McClure was in the fine groove again, for sure.

For damn sure.

* * *

At Highway 90, the Interstate Connecticut thruway, in the glare of the sunlight a state trooper operating a radar trap had drawn blood. He had hauled two speedsters into his net and both were pulled off the road at his waving summons. One of them was the black Lamborghini bearing Marcie Thatcher and Jill Rivers.

Marcie saw him coming and turned on the charm before he could open his mouth. The trooper was young enough to be vulnerable— brand new uniform and all. And women were women. Especially knockouts.

"Really sorry about that little lapse, there, officer," Marcie cooed. "Normally I drive right around the speed limit."

"We all make mistakes," the officer agreed, "but *eighty-eight* is more than a little lapse, miss."

Marcie and Jill, as his head lowered to his

ticket book, had partially unzipped their form-fitting coveralls. Tantalizing acres of abundant cleavage shone in the sun. Marcie moistened her red lips and handed the cop her driver's license. "I *am* sorry," she murmured, letting her voice fall, too. Jill had almost gone all the way. Her twin breasts were ready to charge. The officer glanced up from the offered license, ready to say something, then stopped cold.

He was riveted, reduced to eye-popping wonder.

At that crucial point of events, something new was added.

The white Rolls Royce of the young Sheik, and the mad motorcycle bearing Bradford W. Compton and Shakey Finch, whistled on by, nose to tail. They were running at better than a hundred and ten miles mph. The Rolls engine hummed like a full orchestra, the motorcycle's tiny horn squawked an impudent salute in passing. Soon, both machines disappeared over the next low hill of the roadway.

Still distracted, the patrolman watched them flee from his legal jurisdiction. He shook his head, confused.

"What in the name of Jesus is going on? Everybody is driving like maniacs! I'm the last patrolman between here and the New York State line and I've used up *all* my tickets in the last hour!"

He showed the two girls his empty citation pad.

Jill leaned forward, her mammaries pushing out and down. "It's just another sign of the decline of Western Civilization, officer.''

And still there was more to come.

The gray-primed stock car, bearing David Pearson and Stan Barrett, now hurtled by, the pavement vibrating from its wide-open exhausts. Dave and Stan's tinkering had paid off handsomely. The stock car was clicking on all six, as the old expression goes.

The state policeman had seen enough, and had had enough. Madly running machines and half-naked lady drivers had done him in.

He tore up his last ticket with monumental frustration.

''That's it! Forget it! I'll be damned if I'm going to penalize nice girls like you for a little indiscretion when the road is packed with speed-crazy lunatics!''

''God bless you, sir,'' Marcie Thatcher simpered, and geared the Lamborghini far down the road before Young Law could change his mind.

Jill Rivers laughed in unladylike fashion and zippered up her one-piece. There was always something smart girls could do about everything. In fact, anything! Particularly, two smart girls.

* * *

At Bridgeport, Connecticut Airport, a large cargo plane was idling on the apron of the runway.

Powerful propellors whirled briskly. The Excalibur of Shelly and Manny, the Hollywood duo, came racing into view on a far corner of the runway, and without missing a beat or a change of direction, zoomed up the loading ramp that fed neatly into the side of the cargo monster. On the move, with perfect timing, the cargo door slammed shut and the big metal bird revved up its engines and taxied across the field, pointing its nose West for take-off. Soon, it was running smooth, clearing the hard-packed field and clawing for wild blue yonder. Soon white clouds scudded softly below.

Within the cargo plane, Shelly and Manny were celebrating.

Still seated in the Excalibur, they were laughing with mutual warmth, applauding their own cleverness. Shelly had a long Perfecto cigar clamped between his white teeth. Manny was uncorking a chilled bottle of champagne. Two glasses were ready for filling.

"To us, eh?" Shelly snickered evilly, dark eyes shining.

Manny was pouring, the bubbles rising merrily.

"I would like to propose a toast. To victory through air power! And welcome to the friendly skies . . ." He never finished his sentence.

Something intruded. Or rather, *pro*truded, smashing all crooked dreams of winning this race by underhanded methods.

The ominous, black metallic snout and bulk of an automatic pistol was poking into Shelly's face with unmistakable purpose. Shelly almost lost his suntan and Manny abruptly halted his toast. Their past had caught up with them and the future was questionable.

A third man had joined the planned party, a complete stranger. He loomed into view, materializing from the rear seat of the Excalibur. Loose talk can do that sometimes. Especially in bars where you gloat over drinks about how you're going to win the Cannonball—by beating everybody there by airplane! Especially if the guy who eavesdrops is a worse crook than you are—like this gunman wearing a turtleneck with his face completely covered by a ski mask. Hijacker, all the way.

"I hope you've got a lot of that stuff, Yankee devils," a low, heavily accented voice rasped from behind the mask. "It's going to be a long flight to Libya!"

Libya!. . . Shelly and Manny almost choked. A couple of too-wise city boys taken to the cleaners by a hijacker!

The cargo plane droned onward. But it would be changing its direction soon enough—for Libya, not Redondo Beach.

Scratch two entrants for the Cannonball Memorial Trophy Dash, two would-be winners who had wound up losers before they even started.

* * *

"Look at it this way," J. J. McClure was explaining patiently to a stunned Pamela Glover as the ambulance ploughed westward. "A leisurely trip to California, a day or two in the sunshine, and we'll have you back home. And it's all on us. Who knows? It might even be fun. You could find yourself having a ball."

Pamela kept shaking her pretty, taffy-haired head.

"I can't believe this is happening to me. I mean, this isn't a joke any longer. You could even call it kidnapping."

J. J. ignored that. He was still lost in the advantages. "And just think, if you have any problem with constipation, we've got a fully licensed doctor right on board."

Pamela shuddered. "You guys are *weird!* I want Arthur."

Victor suddenly erupted in his squeaky voice.

"Oh, oh—trouble! The heat's behind us!"

The Leonia exit on Interstate 80 loomed ahead but a New Jersey Highway Patrol car was now running directly behind the ambulance, the eternal light flashing, the inevitable siren moaning its heartbreaking message. J. J. went into action, shouting orders to his crew. Dr. Nicholas Van Helsing immediately mounted an I.V. bottle from the ceiling of the vehicle, while J. J. and Victor policed their own areas, straightened their uniforms, and assumed attitudes of the most serious professionalism. Van Helsing's white doctor's coat was open, revealing his green surgical blouse and stethoscope dangled from his scrawny neck. Pamela Glover looked on in wonder.

"Hey, Pamela," J. J. snapped. "Jump in that stretcher and lie down while we talk to the cops, will you?"

"Why should I help you?" She bridled. "After leaving poor Arthur like that? That was really cruel. Arthur never hurt anybody." A tear wanted to start in one eye. "All he wanted to do was make the Spaceship Earth a groovier place to hang out on. AND he really loved trees."

J. J. knew the signs and how to deal with them. He adopted a more soothing tone of voice and a more solicitous expression.

"Pamela, honey, how about lying down on the stretcher like a good girl?"

"No. It wouldn't be fair to Arthur."

"I believe," Dr. Nicholas Van Helsing said, "I have a solution."

He held up the long, bent travesty of a hypodermic.

"That may be a little dangerous, Doc," J. J. demurred.

"Nonsense. Merely high-potency vitamins. I use them myself."

To prove that claim, he jabbed himself with the needle, leering his ugly leer. Victor scrambled to the door to greet the arriving officers.

Night had come on, dark and star-filled night.

J. J. joined Victor, trying to think of something, fast.

"Hey, guys." J. J. addressed the two sour-faced police officers approaching grimly. He made his voice breezy, full of goodwill and innocence. "What's up?"

The first officer was surly about that.

"What'ya mean—'what's up'? You guys were doing about a hundred and twenty, flashin' lights all over the place. That's what's up!"

Victor put an oar in, grinning with the milk of human kidness. "Well, officers, we're in a hurry. We got a patient in there!"

The second officer was more belligerent than the first. "You was still speedin'!"

J. J. shook his head, woefully. "Our patient . . . she ain't doing too good. . . ."

The first officer softened at that. "Where you headed?"

"L.A. The UCLA Medical Center."

Both officers responded to that one. *"L.A.!!"*

There was a fast silence for a long moment, a shocked one.

"Well, uh . . ." The first officer rallied. "Why . . . why don't you *fly* her?"

Victor had walked around to the side door. "Maybe you better ask the Doc about that."

The opened door revealed Dr. Nicholas Van Helsing, seated beside the stretcher, looking more solemn than an undertaker. Pamela Glover was lying on the stretcher. The dangling I.V. tube trailed down to her arm, beneath the blanket. Van Helsing stirred irritably.

"What's all this? What sort of crude imposition is this?"

"The patient," the first officer said. "Why can't you fly her to L.A.?"

Dr. Nicholas Van Helsing was very abrupt, and superbly equal to the question.

"Cysts on the walls of her lungs. Very rare. Airplanes are only pressurized to ten thousand feet. We've got no choice but to drive her." Again came the odd contrast of cultured words and slovenly aspect. Pamela Glover did not stir but her voice came faintly, from the stretcher. *"Ten thousand feet . . . whoopeee . . ."*

The second officer stirred. "Is that woman all right?"

"The poor thing is in great pain," Dr. Van Helsing admitted. "It causes certain delirious utterances."

"Yeah . . ." Pamela echoed. *"Delirious . . . whoopee . . ."*

The first officer was suspicious again. "She sounds like she's on something."

Victor, feeling the strain of the moment, was beginning to twitch again. His eyeballs began to roll. His chin trembled. J. J., spotting the signs, grabbed his hand and rushed into the breach. He spun on the cops. Helsing had been fine but more was needed—right away!

"Listen, you guys, I've got seventy-two hours to get the Senator's wife—get that—the *Senator's wife*—to California. Time's a-wasting. If you've got problems, let's get 'em settled."

J. J. and Victor were now holding hands. The second officer noticed and arched a suspicious eyebrow. J. J. grinned, sheepishly.

"Uh—we're just good friends, you know what I mean?"

The officer made a face and turned to his partner. "It figures. They said they were going to California. Probably end up on the San Francisco City Council."

The first officer started to walk away, disgusted.

"That isn't my problem. I'm just telling you one thing," he barked over his shoulder at J. J. "While you're in New Jersey, you'd better damn well take it easy."

Victor had calmed down, thanks to J. J.'s strong hand.

"Yessir, officer. You can count on us!"

With that, both he and J. J. clambered back into the ambulance. J. J. put her in gear and zoomed back into the flow of night traffic. The scare was over. It had been close, that time. Too close.

In response to their fright, J. J., Victor and Van Helsing burst into spontaneous mirth. Their laughter filled the vehicle.

"I'll tell you," J. J. chuckled. "That cop was one guy who was headed for cardiac arrest when we told him we were going to California!"

Dr. Van Helsing nodded and Victor sighed, "Pamela was just terrific. . . ."

Van Helsing almost bowed.

"The lady was splendid. She should have her

picture on the cover of the AMA *Journal.*"

"*Oooh . . .*" Pamela Glover crooned. "*Picture on the cover . . . whoopee . . .*"

"Truly," Dr. Van Helsing crowed. "We are in the age of miracles."

And then he toppled over in a dead faint, eyeballs showing whites. And Pamela Glover fainted, too.

Then J. J. McClure and Victor had the answer to the success of the ruse—Pamela had not been a willing partner to the ploy. Van Helsing's hypodermic had pacified her. Those high-potency vitamins will do it every time.

J. J. McClure looked long and hard at Victor. "If I ever ask you where you got that doctor, don't tell me. I don't want to know."

What possible kind of an answer could there be for that refugee from a horror movie!

The ambulance whipped on, J. J. McClure forgetting his troubles with the thrill, the wonder and the marvel of racing. Acceleration was his fix, his very own high-potency vitamins. Always good for a real high for J. J. McClure.

* * *

Arthur J. Foyt, that most misunderstood man, abused, confused and unloved, had found an airport—any airport, he wasn't particular. And a telephone booth. Foyt was not one to ever let the grass grow under his feet, as much as he loved grass. And there were accounts to settle, oh, were there ever! Nobody could make a folly out of a Foyt project, much less make a fool out of Arthur J. Foyt. The 'J' of his initial stood for *Justice*.

His hurried phone call was a masterpiece of Foyt reportage: accurate, indignant and to the point, with a plan for the next move.

". . . it's the Cannonball . . . the damn Cannonball, for sure. Boss, they blasted away right in front of my eyes. . . . Then they kidnapped Pamela Glover . . . like the goddamn Red Brigade or something! . . . but I've got 'em! . . . Ohio . . . yes, Ohio has been notified. . . . They're ready . . . and Missouri, and California! We got 'em! . . . And I'll be there to handle it! Count on it! . . . Now I've gotta catch my flight . . ."

Arthur J. Foyt slammed down the phone and ran for the waiting plane in the night. He stopped for a moment and glanced up. A sky full of stars, a full moon. And somewhere out there was a tree with his name on it—his and Pamela Glover's.

Arthur J. Foyt was not one of those who think about balling their brains out in, under or out of trees. It was just not his way. But this noble man of Nature was not one to turn away a dish like Pamela Glover—with or without a silver platter. He took a deep breath and ran on.

* * *

Under the same canopy of twinkling stars, with the moon still riding high, Seymour Goldfarb was pushing the silvery Aston-Martin DB-6 for all it was worth. His machine was running hard. Goldfarb's chiseled, supremely handsome face was outlined against the expensive instrument panel lights. At his shoulder, the striking brunette snuggled, a kitten content with her lord and master. Or rather, a tigress. She almost was purring within the warmth of Seymour Goldfarb's body.

". . . and after my career in the RAF—" Seymour murmured in his precise English voice, "—a chestful of medals, citations, that sort of thing . . . I played a rather popular character on television . . . a television series . . . still in syndication, you know. . . ."

The brunette raised herself, a bit skeptical of all that, and opened a small cigarette case in her lap. Then she reached for the chrome lighter poking from the fancy dashboard of the Aston-Martin. Seymour Goldfarb caught the movement.

Without taking his eyes away from the road in his headlamp glare, her gripped her lovely arm. "Please, darling. Not that one. We don't want you leaving so shortly—after all, the trip has only just begun, hasn't it?"

She got the message. Her eyes widened and a quick gasp escaped her. After all, she had seen enough Bond movies to know all about gimmicks and gadgets and explosive devices—

Seymour Goldfarb smiled contentedly and settled back in his place at the wheel with a small sigh. This was indeed the Life! The best things that money could buy at one's very fingertips: the finest cars, the richest clothes, the loveliest women, the remotest islands and places of enchantment . . .

And excitement. Very easy to enter car races when you had money.

Thrills. Very easy to pick up women when you looked as he did.

Danger. There was always that, to spice up life, as it were.

Assignments. Ah, yes . . . the lifeblood and heartbeat of the spy's existence. Assignments such as the Cannonball. Yes, truly a contest for champions. And it would be won by a champion, too, a genuine one. Himself, Seymour Goldfarb.

Suddenly, he longed to see M again, that wise old owl of British Intelligence. And Miss Moneypenny—and Q, weapons master—

Seymour Goldfarb sighed again. The brunette had found a light somewhere else for her cigarette. His chain of thought and memory was interrupted by the wafting smoke. His classic nostrils flared.

And then his mind and attention were riveted on the road, again.

A steep grade loomed before him, rising mysteriously in the night as if it were a pathway to those glorious stars above it. He shifted gears and the Aston-Martin throbbed with power. Seymour 'Roger Moore' Goldfarb raced to the stars, dreaming his magnificent dreams.

DURING OPERATION MAINTENANCE

The PDRA was nailed in the heart of Pennsylvania.

Interstate 80 was deserted and inky black but the arresting officer had plenty of light—in the illumination of his patrol car's headlights—to write out a ticket. The loose-jointed Petoski, leaning out his van window, was helpless and grieving.

"I'd really like to explain why we were running so fast, officer."

The officer was reading him the riot act. He resumed writing and growled, "Don't bother. I've heard them all."

"Listen—we were running out of gas so I was speeding up in order to coast to the next gas station."

The officer looked up, writing pen still poised.

"You're right," he admitted.

Petoski smiled, hopefully. "You mean—?"

"You're right. I never heard that one before."

Rir-r-r-rrrrip!

Petoski took the extended ticket.

Marcie Thatcher and Jill Rivers and their black Lamborghini were having their usual amount of better luck, sex being here to stay. The Pennsylvania State Police, halting the racing black car, found too much to condone when the two women were such startling knockouts. 'Twas ever thus. In spite of all reports to the contrary, lawmen are only human, too. Jill Rivers's coveralls, zippered down to the navel, was bound to make a man forget the more important matters at hand.

". . . and just take it a little easier," the officer declared sweetly, "from here on in, will you, girls?"

Jill looked grateful, seductively so.

"Thanks so much, officer. We *really* do appreciate that warning, and remember, if you're ever up in Duluth, be sure to look me up."

The officer, who had already done his share of looking, beamed.

"You can count on that, honey." The beam widened into a leer. "I've got the number."

He was holding up his address book even as Marcie Thatcher and Jill Rivers roared away once more, disappearing into the darkness.

When dawn broke over western Ohio, on Interstate 70, Pamela Glover was groggily reviving in the bumpy ambulance interior. She tried to rise on her elbows, the world still spinning. The first person she saw was that ghoul, Dr. Nicholas Van Helsing. Then handsome J. J.

McClure and the pudgy Victor came into her range of vision. For a long moment, she was fighting for balance. Then all the facts and figures righted themselves, as she realized where she was and all that had happened.

"Gentlemen," Dr. Van Helsing cackled, "the patient is conscious. And so am I. We survived the procedure."

Pamela Glover blanched, eyes popping. She tried not to panic.

"What procedure? If you people laid a finger on me—Oh! My head—" She reached for her throbbing temples.

"Sounds like normal post-operative depression."

"*Operations?*" Pamela's hands flew under the blankets to check the condition of her own body.

Van Helsing smiled his crooked smile.

J. J. McClure rushed in. "It's okay," he soothed Pamela. "We're just kind of fooling around."

Pamela flopped back on the stretcher. "I hope so," she muttered grandly. "My body—is a temple!"

Dr. Van Helsing clucked. "Not to worry, my pet. We are among its most pious worshippers."

The ambulance roared on, eating up Ohio's dust.

Not too far away, the gleaming Subaru, with its team of Japanese drivers, was speeding west.

Both operators had found themselves a couple

of cowboy hats and string bowties. They were accommodating themselves to the American scene and were having the time of their lives.

But their transistor-special was still a dizzy clutter of banks of computers and digital read-outs. Driver Number Two punched a button and a central panel lit up as if by magic. The CRT screen flashed: *Indianapolis, 114 miles; average speed, 81 mph, next fuel stop, Effingham, Illinois.*

Number One Driver, honorably so, showed white teeth in a moon face as he barked in the staccato of his native tongue while his companion nodded admiringly. Translated, he would have sounded something like this:

"These poor shit-kickers have heard about Black Power, People Power, Solar Power, Cold Power and Pucker Power, by Tao, but they ain't heard nuthin' till they've heard about Transistor Power!"

The nation of small people who specialized in small things was pretty damn certain it would win this Cannonball affair with two such drivers and their wonder machine. In the light of this new conquest, maybe the world would forget Pearl Harbor! Finally.

* * *

"Hey, J. J.! Some guys are trying to pull us over. They look like priests—" Victor was at the wheel now, spelling J. J. McClure.

"Priests?" echoed J. J., looking up from a road map at the flashy red Ferrari cruising alongside. Fathers Jamie Blake and Morris Fenderbaum were smiling benignly upward and waving. "In a Ferrari? They must be winning their own Bingo games. Screw 'em. We stop now and we'll hit the rush hour traffic in St. Louis. Keep driving."

"Hey." Victor was indignant. "I'm a Catholic. And so is 'you know who.' "

J. J. realized he had touched a sensitive spot in his fat friend and shrugged. Keep Captain Chaos happy—and in the pouch at Victor's belt.

"All right, all right. Pull over and see what they want."

The ambulance and the Ferrari meshed at roadside, halting parallel to each other. The priests got out and approached the ambulance, exuding benevolence. Father Jamie Blake bore down on J. J. Unnoticed, Father Morris Fenderbaum slithered around the side of the ambulance and disappeared.

"We appreciate your stopping, my son. Whenever we see an ambulance, we try to bless the patient." Father Blake was geniality itself.

Victor was smiling broadly at sight of this man of religion. It seemed a wonderful omen of victory to Victor, as if God were personally blessing the enterprise.

"That's really nice, Father," J. J. said. "But actually our patient is a Zen Buddhist."

"It matters not. The heart of the Lord is wide and loving—"

"Sure, sure."

"The patient's faith has no bearing on us. We'd still like to say a few words over her."

J. J. shuffled a little and finally gave up. One look at Victor's beatific face told him it was worth it.

"Okay, Father, but why don't you do it right from there? We've got quite a ways to go. We're in a little bit of a hurry."

"Certainly, my son."

Father Blake began a resonant litany of incantations and mumblings at the front window of the ambulance, too earnest to be for real. Meanwhile, the unseen Fenderbaum had squirmed his wiry slip of a body under the vehicle and engaged himself in a bit of sabotage. As he finally wriggled out, he smoothly slashed the left rear tire with a switchblade. J. J., anxious to be gone, did not notice the gypsy glitter in Jamie Blake's eye. The phony priest's act was good enough in a pinch.

". . . and bless these heroic, selfless paramedics who care for this lovely lady, dear Lord. *Amen . . .*"

Victor, completely taken in by the entire ceremony, brushed a tear from his eye. And crossed himself vigorously.

"Gee, thanks, Father, that was terrific!"

The priests waved a final blessing, and walked back to their Ferrari. But their celerity puzzled J. J. His suspicions were only too sadly confirmed when Blake and Fenderbaum literally leaped into the vehicle, Blake geared expertly, and the red car shot away from the scene like greased lightning. Morris Fenderbaum, black face glowing with a toothy smile, was leaning from the seat window, bellowing:

"So long, *putzes!* Why don't you drive that thing back to the junkyard where you found it!"

Bingo, eh? And *Up Yours!*

J. J. and Victor exchanged confused glances.

And thanks to the ministrations of Morris Fenderbaum, when Victor tried to move the ambulance ahead again, it did not budge. They found the trouble all too soon. As J. J. fingered the slashed left rear tire, he noticed the steady trickle of transmission fluid forming a puddle in the roadway. Fenderbaum had struck, and struck well. Victor stamped up and down in a rage, twitching again. "What's going on here?" he cried out petulantly. J. J.'s jaw hardened, his eyes narrowed and his moustache fairly bristled.

"I'll tell you what's going on, here. Those guys . . . they weren't Fathers . . . they were *Mothers!"*

Amen to that, sons.

The sun was well up now, bathing the countryside in enough daylight to see just how stupid they had been. It was enough to make a man really go to the Devil. . . .

* * *

The morning rush-hour traffic, brought to a crawl in an Interstate tangle across the Mississippi River at St. Louis, failed to halt the Aston-Martin as it slipped deftly from lane to lane. St. Louis was a motorized madhouse, the immense Gateway Arch towering above the city skyline like some monster magnet, drawing all four-wheeled things to its base.

Seymour Goldfarb, dauntless and impeccable as ever, was regaling yet another beautiful lady with tales of his incredible lifetime, the stunning brunette having been replaced somewhere along the route. This one, a golden-haired blonde of generous proportions, was plucking grapes and feeding them to Goldfarb even as he drove. From time to time, he topped off the grapes with a sip of champagne from a dainty cocktail glass. The full life was endless. The loaded picnic hamper rocked gently against the plush back seat. Again, a feminine hand reached for the dashboard lighter. Goldfarb gently pushed the tapering fingers away, his debonair glow pure Roger Moore.

". . . so there you have it. A rather simple story actually. International film star, Casanova, ruthless assassin, philosopher, poet, living legend. Really little more than your run-of-the-mill Renaissance man . . ." He smiled boyishly.

"I need a light for my cigarette," the blonde

whimpered.

"Please, darling. Not that button. I'm afraid this car is full of surprises."

He fired the cigarette with a pocket lighter from his tuxedo.

". . . as I was saying . . . when that other chap ceased to want to be in the films, they immediately came to me. In fact, I'd been their first choice from the beginning. . . ."

Behind him, the white Rolls Royce was closing in, horn blasting.

The young Sheik and company had tailgated the Aston-Martin for the last twenty miles, taking advantage of the silver bellwether's maneuvering. Seymour Goldfarb was oblivious—there was so much to tell the blonde about himself. . . .

Miles later, in what passed as central Missouri, the Aston-Martin and the Rolls Royce ran into a knot of trucks—*heavy* trucks, semis and trailer monsters—a convoy of eighteen-wheelers. The CB airwaves crackled with a continuing barrage of the usual knights-of-the-open road chatter: *four-tens* and *double eighty-eights* and *Charlie* and *beaver patrol* jargon. . . .

". . . *ten-fer, dontcha know . . . Cotton-pickin' bears in that chicken coop . . . Roger on that, fer sher . . . Howzit look over your donkey . . .*"

And the reply:

". . . *keep an eyeball out for that Smokey on the westbound side, dontcha know . . . hey, how about the driver one time in that silver dollar roller skate . . . Hey, driver, gotcher ears on? . . .*"

All of which pained Seymour Goldfarb no end. His ears ached from this assault on his mother tongue. *Really!*

He unhooked his own CB and fought back.

"See here, you chaps, you are going to have to speak much more clearly and in the King's English if you expect us to converse on the wireless. . . ."

What followed that declaration over the CB radios could not have been reprinted in any family magazine.

On Interstate 44 in Missouri, a superfast pit stop was in order for the ambulance, which had gotten rolling again after Victor made repairs. J. J. found the gasoline station and was quick-drawing two gasoline hoses while Victor frantically loaded cans of transmission fluid into the filler neck. A baffled attendant stood by, watching. Pamela Glover sprinted for the Ladies' Room, heeding Mother Nature's call, followed by Dr. Nicholas Van Helsing. All the way into the room, which is No Man's Land. Pamela Glover was aghast.

"You can't come in here! You're a guy!"

The good doctor was not dismayed. Sex was the furthest from his mind.

"I am also a physician. If I may be permitted an indelicacy, if you've seen one, you've seen them all." He squirmed impatiently.

Pamela was puzzled, but conceded. "Well, okay, if you put it that way."

The door to the Ladies' Room banged shut.

Meanwhile, Shakey Finch and Bradford W. Compton that very moment pulled into the same gas station on their motorcycle. They quickly filled up with gas and exchanged places at the wheel. Compton was now driving, Finch rode the pommel behind him. But not before readjusting the blond wig again and straightening the JUST MARRIED sign. Shakey, alas, carried weight far too substantial for mere mortals, much less a racing Suzuki. The bike's rear wheel wobbled, and Compton clung to the handlebars, fighting for counterbalance. Fat Shakey outweighed all considerations. The bike tilted precariously. The sign swayed. The gleaming Suzuki was off at a wobble.

J. J. had the ambulance ready to go.

He handed the attendant a wad of bills, refused change and mounted up. But as he did so, he spotted in his rearview mirror the approach of a red Ferrari with its holy carload. Smiling, J. J. Mc Clure accelerated hard. Just in time, too—Dr. Van Helsing and Pamela with two seconds to spare, leaped into the vehicle puffing after the exertions of their mutual mission.

The ambulance peeled out as the Ferrari turned into the station.

They needed gas, too, the good Fathers.

Gas is the one requisite of every automotive vehicle—give or take a little chicken crap—no matter what make, what year, what amount of money or what ambition goes into its production.

Father Morris Fenderbaum rushed to the phone booth. Father Jamie Blake handled the pumps and then sat impatiently blipping the engine as his little black compatriot dawdled on the horn.

"Speed it up, short stuff," Blake howled. "Time's awasting!"

"Cool it, glands," Fenderbaum called. "I get hold of the Greek and we all make money—including you, you hockey puck!" His Las Vegas connection finally connected. "Greek? Greek? . . . hey, it's me, Fenderbaum, you fathead! Listen, you wanta go *another* ten G's?"

Through the glass door of the booth, Fenderbaum could see the Subaru zipping across the Interstate median, braking hard, U-turning, and flying off in the direction from whence it had come. Fenderbaum grinned maliciously, waggling his jaw. The slanties were sure-fire losers, for his dough. With disdain and delight, he watched the wild Subaru twist out of sight, burning rubber.

"And put another five on the Japs. That they *don't* finish until December seventh!"

Chuckling, he hung up on the sputtering Greek and returned to Blake and the Ferrari. Blake grimaced, geared, accelerated and yowled off into the distance. His Grand Prix skills were getting a royal workout.

The Cannonball was boiling down; the clutter was on them all. There was no spread yet, no good distance between all the madly churning, competing wheels. But there was still plenty of time. Plenty of moving, operating space. Wait, just wait.

Morris Fenderbaum was feeling better than he had in a long time.

Maybe the priest outfit *was* helping?

You never could tell—

* * *

A Missouri highway patrol car, parked on the Interstate median, suddenly found an ambulance pulling up alongside. J. J. McClure smiled from the driver's side, boyishly and good-naturedly. The big cop at the wheel of the patrol car blinked at him.

J. J. said, "Excuse me, officer. I'd like to ask you something. Do you folks take your law and order seriously around here?"

"Are you kidding?" The cop jerked a thumb at the huge billboard just behind him, at roadside. It seemed to be a re-election poster for none other than BOB 'Kill A Commie' CONROY, and beneath the enormous photo of a man in a riot helmet and sunglasses, flamed the vote-collecting slogan: GOD, GUNS AND GUTS KEEP US SAFE FROM THE HIPPIE NUTS. J. J. surveyed the billboard with the proper amount of respect —for the cop's benefit.

"Sorry I asked."

"Why'd you want to know?"

J. J. smiled, again. "You might want to keep your eyeballs peeled for a red Ferrari that's going to come through here in a few minutes."

The cop squinted. Always suspicion from cops. "Why's that?"

"We've got one of their victims in here."

"Victim?"

"Child molesters. Escaped from a nuthouse in Dayton, Ohio. Stole the Ferrari from this poor child's father." J. J. motioned behind him, "Worst part is, they always do it when they're dressed up like priests. Guess it's kinkier that way."

That was enough for any cop. This one was a sight for J. J.'s bleary eyes.

"Goddamn, that's sick!" He started up his engine, turned on his flashers. "I'll handle it from here! Don't worry."

"Oh, yeah," J. J. threw in, as if it were but an afterthought. "I understand they're armed."

The cop patted the shotgun on his dashboard, almost chortling. "Damn, I hope they are. It'll give me an excuse!"

J. J. took off, satisfied, noting with great glee and satisfaction that the Ferrari in question was just coming up, heading directly toward the police car with the flashing lights. He could not resist a parting gesture. He was only human, after all. He leaned from his cab and tossed a wave of his hand at the arriving Ferrari. And put both fingers into it, too, in the universal signal known all around the world as *Up Yours!*

It was too bad he could not stick around to see the fireworks. He would have enjoyed it immensely.

In no time at all, the righteous cop had Fathers Fenderbaum and Blake dismounted, stomachs pressed against the low roof of the Ferrari, their hands locked behind their necks while he asked for instructions over his police radio. The shotgun, larger than life, was leveled at their unsaintly middles.

Fenderbaum had hit the ceiling—and stayed there. . . .

"You dummy! I hope you aren't a Catholic. When the Archbishop hears about this, he's gonna make sure you end up in a place where you'll need asbestos underwear!"

Father Blake was much smarter than Father Fenderbaum. His smile was truly Christian and forgiving.

"Please don't mind him, officer. He's been locked up in a monastery for six years. He's a little . . ."

"Shut up, you perverts!" the cop bellowed. "Six years is gonna seem like a summer vacation when the State of Missouri gets through with you—you won't be going to any summer camp!"

The good Fathers shuddered in unison. They knew an angry cop when they saw one. And heard one.

The bastard in the ambulance had pulled a fast one!

Down the road a piece, J. J. McClure listened as Victor, busy with the CB, was passing on the road talk. Pamela and Dr. Nicholas Van Helsing were sleeping like kids in the rear of the ambulance. J. J. liked the way Pamela looked sleeping. Like a big and beautiful blond doll. But Victor's news was a mite depressing.

"There's a lot of talk about a roadblock ahead. It's all over the CB. What do you think?"

"I think we're in deep shit. That oil cooler leak is gettin' worse, thanks to those phony Fathers. Lookit that temperature—" He indicated the gauge before him. "The thing is getting ready to blow unless we fix that leak."

"Yeah, and the roadblock, too."

"Gimme a minute to gather my thoughts."

Before him loomed a massive flatbed truck running in the slow lane. In seconds, the ambulance would overtake it. J. J. nodded.

"I just gathered 'em. Gimme that mike."

Victor looked on, curious and eager, as J. J. McClure swept the hand mike from his pudgy paw and began to talk rapidly.

Victor smiled wide. He got the whole picture that second. Old J. J. was coming through again, loud and clear. Like a line drive between second and third base.

Nearly as good as Captain Chaos—than whom there was none better, of course. Still, J. J. was a winner!

* * *

Arthur J. Foyt, that man on the move, had been busy too.

Now, with the complete and wholehearted co-operation of the Missouri highway patrol, he had organized a mammoth roadblock through which no outlaw vehicle could have a hope of sneaking through. The westbound lane of the freeway was clogged with traffic. Long lines of cars of every description were halted, checked out and examined. In the midst of the mass, the Aston-Martin gleamed, the Polish Racing Drivers of America panel truck, the ugly gray stock car.

Arthur J. Foyt, spotted the flashy, silver Aston-Martin and smelled pay dirt. Smiling wide, he strode briskly toward it. He was carrying his pad with the list of license plate numbers. Thorough, was Arthur J. Foyt. But he didn't know he was up against James Bond.

Seymour Goldfarb placed a manicured fingertip on a button in the dashboard. The glorious redhead at his side, still another beautiful lady, stifled a yawn.

Magically, silently, the Aston-Martin's license plate flipped from MISSOURI to VERMONT. Good old Q, that wizard of devices.

Foyt checked himself, halting, and then checking his pad for the Aston-Martin number he had spotted the day before. No good. It was not there. Seymour Goldfarb smiled charmingly

151

as he cruised by, past Foyt's disgruntled wave-through. But as the Aston passed, Foyt's eyes gleamed anew. Coming up in the line of cars was the familiar ugly gray stock car that belonged to Stan Barrett and David Pearson.

Foyt flagged them to a halt. "Where are you men headed?"

"Oh, we was goin' out to get us a pack of cigarettes."

"With North Carolina plates?—You drive all the way to Missouri for cigarettes?"

One of the highway patrolman had been staring at the stock car, examining the gray primer paint through narrowed eyes. The paint had begun to peel away, disastrously, revealing a faint outline of a giant number on the right-side door. Triumphantly, the patrolman called Foyt to his side. Our man immediately reacted. He scraped at the paint, peeling more away, until the complete number was produced. Arthur J. Foyt whooped.

"Seize these men! They're Cannonballers for sure."

Stan Barrett and David Pearson did not even try to run.

In that cluster of cars with so many cops, it would have been futile. So they allowed them-selves to be hauled from the stock car and hand-cuffed. Justice had triumphed, as far as Arthur J. Foyt was concerned. After all, Justice was his middle name! He turned to one of the officers as the two speedsters were being hauled away and rubbed his palms together in high glee. "Now!

The good guys strike back!'' he rumbled.

It was turning out to be his day, all around.

His eagle eye, questing for more victims, spied the bulky PDRA van mired in the heaviest part of the traffic jam. His heart soared.

He barely gave a glance to the big Kenworth flatbed truck he passed, the one that carried what seemed to be a cowboy trailer.

He scurried forward, threading his way between vehicles.

On the trailer was a large lump covered over by heavy tarpaulin. Had Arthur J. Foyt smelled trouble and raised the canvas covering, he would have found a large white ambulance filled to overflowing with the sort of folks he so dearly wanted to stop dead in their tracks, *and* his lovely Pamela. But this one he missed—the one he wanted most.

Lying beneath the ambulance, Victor was hard at work, frantically working on the faulty transmission, rapping with a socket wrench and not being too quiet about it, considering the mob outside the truck.

"Dammit, Victor, be quiet!'' J. J. hissed. "You're gonna blow our cover.''

"Sorry, J. J.'' Victor was puffing. "This isn't exactly a desk job down here, you know.''

The interior of the ambulance was a litter of empty transmission cans, tools, maps, candy wrappers and rumpled clothes. All semblance of the medical scam had been discarded in a wash of fatigue and transmission troubles. Dr.

Nicholas Van Helsing was sitting in the front seat of the ambulance, staring ahead. Either that or he was asleep—who could really tell? Besides, he didn't matter. He was only window-dressing.

J. J. unearthed a couple of badly mashed sandwiches out of the cooler and handed one to Pamela Glover. For once, she seemed softer and less blank. Her eyes were winningly warm and womanly.

"Here. You want one?" had been J. J.'s offer.

"Thanks. I appreciate that. You look tired."

"More frustrated. If Victor can't fix that leak, the transmission will probably blow before we get there."

"Are we going to win?"

"Sure. We still got a chance. No guessing what's happening to the other guys." J. J. had sold the Kenworth driver a lovely bill of goods. Now, the guy was helping them run in the Cannonball. And dodge the Law.

Pamela Glover looked at him, tenderly. She was a trifle confused.

"You know, aside from you guys kidnapping me, I've got to admit you've behaved like real gentlemen."

"What'd you expect?" J. J. gnawed at his sandwich.

"Oh, maybe a gang rape."

"Hey, we're racers," J. J. protested. "Not rapers."

"But why?"

"Why, what?"

154

"Why all this speed, all this risk, all this—trouble?"

J. J. smiled. "You ever do anything just for the hell of it?"

"I suppose so."

"Well, that's what this is all about. Just for the hell of it."

She had not touched her sandwich, rolling it between her hands, still looking just at him.

"It still seems weird to me—but I got to admit, it is kind of wild racing across the country and everything, with all those people trying to stop you." She began to unwrap her sandwich.

J. J. nodded, eyes glowing suddenly.

"You know, my old man worked forty-six years in a foundry. He saved up all his money all his life so he could buy a little fishing camp down on the Pee Dee River in North Carolina. He and my mom sold their house and the day they were moving out, he got a heart attack. Keeled over and died. And what was all that saving for?" He answered his own question vehemently. "For nothing."

"I guess you just never know—"

"Exactly. I decided right then and there I wasn't going to wait for my kicks. You never know when the big croupier in the sky is gonna call your number. That's basically why I'm running the Cannonball. It's one of the last great adventures and I'm gonna get my share of the gusto while I can."

Pamela Glover shivered, ecstatic. "That's deep," she murmured. "Really deep."

J. J. McClure grinned. "What would you think about me climbing in that rack with you for a little while?" He had pointed to the long, low all-purpose stretcher.

Pamela Glover did not titter. Nor did she even sound giddy or silly when she replied, softly; "That's really a swell idea. I thought you'd never ask."

Arthur J. Foyt would not only have been shocked out of his underwear, he never would have forgiven her.

Meanwhile, scratch Stan Barrett and David Pearson from the Cannonball. Gone with the Arthur J. Foyt wind.

And then there were more dropouts to come, Foyt was seeing to that, too, bless his company hide.

* * *

As the flatbed Kenworth truck chugged toward freedom with a mechanic working, a doctor maybe sleeping and two lovers loving, Arthur J. Foyt had descended righteously and wrathfully on the PDRA, the Polish Racing Drivers of America, one Petoski and Company, in particular. Petoski took it like a man—he went down fighting. No less was expected of him. This, after all, was front line!

Foyt snarled at his heroic stance. "You guys

didn't really think you could make it, did you? We'll get the whole lot of you, now."

"Not here, you won't," Petoski was going down with all the flags flying, particularly the Polish flag. "The word is out about your little roadblock. They're talkin' it all up and down the super slab. We just got stuck in the jam-up and couldn't turn around. But all the guys behind us have jumped off, taken different routes. They're long gone, buddy."

Foyt was squinting again. Anger always affected his eyes.

"And you call yourself Americans . . ."

Petoski had the lights of eagles in his eyes. "Naw, naw, we call ourselves *Polacks*. Can't you read the sign?"

Arthur J. Foyt quit in disgust. It was hopeless talking to such men. He ignored Petoski's finger pointing to the emblem on his van, the PDRA symbol, and turned away to the policeman at his side. "Take these criminals away," he commanded.

Scratch Petoski and Company from the Cannonball, too. Smaller and smaller the list . . . the roll diminishing.

When Petoski did not move, Arthur J. Foyt exploded. He hauled Petoski away from the wheel of his van, pulling him to the pavement. But the van was still in gear. And before anyone—Foyt, Petoski and his co-driver, or the burly cop backing up all of Foyt's play—could stop it, the heavy van rolled down the embankment. Within five fiery seconds, it exploded with

157

a thunderous roar, bursting into flames somewhere below as the gasoline tank touched off. All that gas.

The burly cop whirled on Arthur J. Foyt, eyeballs bulging. "All right, asshole," he roared. "Let me see *your* license!"

Arthur J. Foyt closed his eyes.

The Cannonball had run almost half the course now. Some of the drivers would have reached clear across the state of Missouri, nearly a day had gone by—how many hours had it been?—sixteen, seventeen, eighteen?

Far away, the white ambulance had been unloaded from the flatbed. J. J. McClure shook hands with their new amigo, and Victor, wiping his hands free of greasy mechanic's work, was once more climbing behind the wheel.

Pamela Glover, eyes shining, was silent and thoughtful.

Dr. Nicholas Van Helsing was trying to clean his fingernails.

Oklahoma was next on the tortuous route to the Portofino Inn in Redondo Beach, California.

Bradford W. Compton and Shakey Finch were enduring all the torments of a lifetime in this one race. Even as they zoomed along, the machine teetered precariously, fairly riding on one wheel under the weight of the bulky Finch. Compton was hard-put to keep his course straight and even, much less safe.

"You should have given up eating, Shakey!" he roared to the rear. "No way," Shakey shouted in his ear. "I wanna die on a full stomach. Besides, pizza is good for you. Greatest junk food there is!"

The motorbike galloped daringly onward, passing heavier vehicles.

Compton and Finch were making great time.

The young Sheik, motoring like the True Son of the Desert he was—far more familiar with camels than cars—came screeching up in the dead of night to a gas station. There, a bewildered, big-breasted attendant, a sight to delight any Arab's harem eye, leaned forward to take the Sheik's order. His teeth gleamed in the darkness of his beard as he studied the gleaming décolletage before him, a feast for any man's eyes, let alone a Sheik.

"What can I do for you, sir?" asked the beauteous gas attendant, in her form-fitting jeans and bursting uniform blouse. He was many things but the Sheik was not a blind man. No, verily!

"By Allah, this chariot of the gods has left your poor police department far behind! My gasoline tanks are thirsty. Kindly fill them to overflowing, lovely one."

It took all kinds of customers to make a business. The doll-faced attendant shrugged and obeyed him.

While the dusty Rolls Royce was being tended to, the tired, utterly worn bodyguards of the Sheik caught some shut-eye in the rear of the air-conditioned Rolls. When the attendant came back for the Sheik's money, it was only to find the dark-bearded face in rapt concentration on her full figure. The Sheik's black-eyed stare was pure lechery.

The Sheik quickly slipped one of the many jewel-encrusted rings off his brown finger and extended it to her.

"I will come back for you, angel of delight. You will honor my harem. Your beauty much favors these eyes."

"Come again?" After all, a man with a beard in a white Rolls Royce, dressed in a flowing *burnoose,* isn't all that common.

"Yes, you will do. Thy beauty will sparkle like the stars in Islam's sky. Come—take this! A token of my deep regard—"

"Huh?"

The ring was thrust into her hand. The Sheik's other hand closed over hers, cupping it. He pressed her flesh warmly, still showing his mouth full of white teeth. The attendant pulled back, in alarm.

"I shall return," declared the young Sheik, gearing up again with a roar of engine power. "But first, Burning Bright, I must win this Cannonball. On my return, I shall come for you. Be ready!"

Before she could sputter a reply or wonder what to do with a priceless ring in payment for gasoline, he was backing up, zooming off. And then he stopped again, and backed up, screeching again to a stop. Now, it was an unbelievably thick wad of green American money he was slamming into her hand.

"This too is yours. All women who fill my harem deserve untold wealth and comfort. It is the will of Allah. It is my will. Dress yourself, oh, Angel! Bedeck and adorn thy beauty as befits my house!"

"Huh?" The poor girl was now completely stunned.

The dark eyes flashed again, the teeth sparkled and the sharp goatee wagged with approval.

"I go, my love! To win the Cannonball and bring honor to the Sword of Islam. *Ya illah, Allah!*"

With that, the Rolls was off, the window sliding upward, and the Son of the Desert was gone as rapidly as he had come. Tires squealed, the engine thundered and the Rolls was a white streak bulleting back down the darkened highway.

It was too much, too soon, for the slick chick of a gas attendant. Far too much. She had never been out of the state of Oklahoma.

She sagged against the nearest gas pump, almost swooning.

Clutched in both hands was a ring worth at least seventy thousand dollars on the open market, and green bills totalling a round thousand. A once-in-any-lifetime windfall.

Dazed, bosom heaving, she watched the tail lights of the Rolls Royce vanish in the night. It was enough to make a girl believe in God again, by cracky!

Pamela Glover was suddenly discovering that all the world was a man, one very particular and one very special man. His name was J. J. McClure, and he was tall, muscular and handsome with a real groove of a moustache. But more than that—he was a *nice* man. Very nice. Nicer than anyone she had ever known.

"J. J.," she whispered fervently in the darkened rear of the racing ambulance. "Wanna know something?"

"Yeah, Beauty," he whispered in her ear. "Lay it on me."

Pamela Glover sighed to the roots of her heaven.

"I never knew it could be so good. Without trees, I mean . . ."

J. J. smiled happily and gathered her into his arms, again.

Up front, Victor was driving beautifully, too. . . .

"—and then, Darling, they seemed to want my special services in a number of those spy films. You know the sort of thing. Master villains out to rule the world, secret agent, beautiful women, all manner of death-dealing devices—"

Seymour Goldfarb sighed volubly, sipping champagne as he tooled the Aston-Martin expertly at a speed far above and beyond the legal fifty-five. The interior of the car was like a scented boudoir, lit with the soft glow of the dashboard.

The brunette with the Cleopatra bangs could not get over her luck. Her eyes continued to marvel at this handsome, rich stranger. She leaned against his strong shoulder, gushing out her wonder. "Gee, nobody would ever believe it. Me and you! A famous guy like you!"

Goldfarb continued unabated, the wheel in complete servitude to his deft hand.

". . . of course, the films made an extraordinary amount of money. Boffo box-office and all that. And then they asked me to go to Egypt and there we filmed 'The Fly That Bugged Me.' Quite an epic that."

"Go on, more, more!"

"Well, it was the same old thing. Sensational. But I must say to this very day I cannot abide the taste of dates. . . ."

"Gee. You're wonderful. Wait till I tell the girls at the club. They're just not going to believe me!"

Without taking his keen eyes off the strip of roadway, Seymour Goldfarb pecked at the naked arm entwining his shoulder.

"What will you tell them, Darling?"

"Why, about you. And me. And all this! Gee, I saw all those pictures and I loved them. Who would ever think that one day you would walk into my life. You!"

"Yes. Little Ole Me."

"I still can't get over it. I just can't believe my luck. Me—riding in a car with *George*

Hamilton!"

"George Hamilton?" Seymour Goldfarb echoed, with the bubble bursting right before his eyes.

But that was not all that was bursting. From behind them came the unmistakable whine and keen of a police siren. The rearview mirror told him that this one was getting a little close for comfort. Sighing again, Seymour reached for the dashboard. Cleopatra giggled as she saw the gesture; she *had* seen the movies.

"Which one is it going to be? The rockets? The machine guns?"

"Oil slick," Seymour Goldfarb murmured coolly and pushed the dash button, monitored the console box at his side with its array of inviting buttons.

Within seconds, a blinding spray of viscous fluid shot from the rear of the Aston-Martin, inundating the roadway behind him. The police vehicle didn't have a chance. Its wheels hit the slick surface and in no time at all, the machine was slewing wildly out of control. It ran off the highway and into the nearest tree. But, it seemed, there were others.

They careened around the spreading slick, and kept on coming. Goldfarb's oil well had run dry. The brunette bounced up and down excitedly.

"Patience, my dear." Goldfarb smiled and poked down at one more colored button. The results were as magical as the oil slick. There was no end to the wonders of Q's little toys for grown-up spies and agents.

The world got darker. A billowing, slip-streaming wall of smoke issued from the Aston-Martin's tailpipe. Thick, bilious, choking, blinding fumes.

Brakes screamed, rubber tires screeched as the police drivers sought the highway before them. It was useless. The patrol cars reeled off the road, lurching to a dead stop before they hit anything. The Aston-Martin raced on alone.

"Oh, honey—it worked—it worked!" The brunette gushed.

"Of course it did. Why should you think that it wouldn't?"

"What a man—I—" The brunette began to cough. Violently. She was sputtering. Seymour Goldfarb's eyes arched in surprise. Something was wrong. The black smoke wasn't behaving itself—not at all.

Instead of going out, it was coming in as well! Reversing itself, filling the interior of the Aston-Martin. Then the silvery car was flying straight ahead in an enveloping cloud of darkness. The brunette panicked, tearing at his shoulder and crying out in terror.

But Seymour Goldfarb did not lose his cool.

Men who lose their cool cannot win the Cannonball.

"Darling," he said easily, as he fought the wheel. "Do roll up the windows, will you? After all, there are limits even to my powers. We mustn't overdo it, you know. . . ."

Ian Fleming would have loved Seymour Goldfarb.

STRETCH DRIVE

The atmosphere was turgid with the roar of wheels and motors. Interstate 40, that glaring ribbon of roadway that spans the continent from East to West, was under seige from the black Lamborghini running on a wide-open throttle. Predictably, the state police were hot on Marcie Thatcher's trail. Using the evasive tactics of a fox on the run, the Countach car darted up an off-ramp and back down the other side, but it was no use. This Oklahoma state trooper was a fine driver, too, and hot on the trail. The Lamborghini had to stop, defeated. Mechanically, Marcie unzipped her form-fitting coveralls and told Jill to play it cool. "Let me take care of this poor dummy."

She turned to the driver's side window and put on her most seductive smile. The come-hither look on her face, coupled with the long V of the unzipped suit, was electrifying.

Jill watched, puzzled, as Marcie's expression changed to one of shock—and dejection.

The arresting officer, approaching officiously, was a stern-looking but very attractive highway patrolwoman.

"Er, good day, officer," Marcie Thatcher said, sheepishly.

"Howdy, hot pants." The female copper assumed a sarcastic air, noting the plunging zipper-line. "You wouldn't have a driver's license hidden in there anywhere, would you?"

Jill Rivers slumped against the cushioned seat and muttered under her breath. Marcie Thatcher fumbled helplessly for the required license. The uniformed female waited patiently, losing neither her sarcasm nor her smile. She had all the time in the world.

Marcie Thatcher and Jill Rivers didn't.

The Lamborghini stood dead and still in the roadway. Not going anywhere, not just yet.

Mad Dog and Batman, in the pickup truck, ran into the long line of semis as they lumbered like a herd of elephants up a long hill on the Interstate 40 in the Texas Panhandle. The pickup was blinking its riding lights in an impressive display of candlepower. The CB radio was wide open, alive with chatter; Batman was desperate for information.

"Better watch out," a truck driver's voice broke in, real friendly and neighborlike. *"Your pick 'em-up is gonna be bear bait for sure. . . ."*

Another truck driver bass broke in: *"Better back it down, driver . . ."*

Batman answered over his own mike: ". . . we definitely appreciate you guys worrying about us like that, but we be in a little bit of a hurry. You see, we're running a little protest against the double-nickel . . ."

"*Whoopee!*" The trucker's voice chortled. "*To hell with that double-nickel! Come on, drivers, we gonna help little snowplow keep the hammer down. Come on, come on, pick 'em up!*"

Translation: the *double-nickel* was the fifty-five miles an hour speed limit. No driver in the world likes that one. Anyone who fought it or tried to get rid of it was good enough for truckers. Batman had told them exactly what they wanted to hear, so they were all on the pickup truck's side, now. Which was as good as life insurance.

In a lockstep formation, the semis shifted into the right lane with their turn signals flashing in the growing dusk and their headlights dipped in a full salute. The convoy had formed a solid front.

Batman had gotten himself and Mad Dog interference, as it were, for any beaver patrols they might run into.

Night was coming on, black night that can hide so many things—so many machines. A night that blanketed Texas and New Mexico, all good news for the Cannonballers, unburdened for the duration of the cares and responsibilities of ordinary folk.

The Arab Sheik and his yawning bodyguards were swilling black coffee at a desolate gas station as the white Rolls Royce waited like a beast at bay.

Shakey Finch tinkered with the motorcycle engine as Bradford W. Compton trained a flashlight down at the trouble spot. They were hidden in a copse of trees just off the roadway. The green grass and the thick foliage was making Shakey sneeze. His sinuses again. Compton still had the crease in his trousers. There are very few things that get the Comptons of this world down.

The flashlights of a patrol car illuminated the long arm of the Law writing up a citation.

A driving team changed tires in an Eveready gleam.

Jill Rivers drove while Marcie Thatcher slept, curled like a sexy kitten at her side. The Lamborghini looked like Batmobile in the darkness. A police car's flashing lights tried to pick them up, but Jill raced on, eluding pursuit.

Batman and Mad Dog walked to an Interstate underpass, and stood contemplative; two thin streams, silhouetted against the lights of passing traffic, splashed onto the asphalt.

Seymour Goldfarb continued driving, continued sipping champagne and continued regaling his latest riding companion with tales of the Great Man and the Great Life he had led. Casanova, indeed. The Aston-Martin ran like a run in cheap hose. It was a dream machine on wheels, in more ways than one. Ask Mother Goldfarb, if you ever see her.

The white ambulance cruised cautiously down a deserted main street, a Western town somewhere in the nowhere. A local Smokey was parked in the lights of an all-night diner. J. J. McClure wanted no more confrontations with police cars. He had had his fill. His traveling companions dittoed the sentiment and didn't complain when he drove carefully until he cleared town. Then he opened up again, deep, full throttle.

The Japanese sportscar, the pride of Subaru, was running with all systems go, night or no night. The computers were humming, the lights were flashing on the board. The central readout console locked in on their exact position and flashed an eerie computerized road map of their projected route. The electronic screen read: ENTERING GALLUP, NEW MEXICO, along with the usual readings of position, speed, elapsed time, miles per gallon, remaining fuel . . .

When the Subaru sped past the next road sign, the rocketing vehicle screeched to a braking halt, stopped, made a wild, sweeping U-turn and bulleted off in the opposite direction, with a whine of wheels and engine.

The road sign said: EL PASO, TEXAS.

Banzai!

In other trucks, cars, what-have-you, crewmen curled up like weary children, sleeping soundly through any chaos, amongst the litter of maps, coke bottles, half-eaten sandwiches. But there was a lot of race left, a whole lot of Cannonball, and who knew what the next hours would bring?

* * *

Victor was spelling J. J. Mc Clure at the wheel
once more. He wasn't too fond of night driving
but J. J. was worn out. He was dozing in the
back now, along with the also sleeping Dr.
Nicholas Van Helsing. It was raining, too. The
wipers slashed across the windshield in a mad-
dening rhythmic squeak, like two-stepping mice.
He thought sadly of his gerbils and home. . . .

Just ahead, the Lamborghini's tail lights were
disappearing in the blackness. Victor growled
unhappily.

"If *he* was driving, they'd never run away
from us like that."

Sitting next to him, Pamela Glover stirred.
"Victor, I don't know how to say this." She
didn't want to hurt his feelings, he was a nice
man. "But isn't it a little weird having that other
guy running around inside your head like that?"

Victor wagged his head. "But he's not *in*
here—" He pointed to his balding head. "He's
out there, somewhere. Helping people. He's
always helping people."

"How'd he find you? I mean, why does he
help you and not me?"

Victor could see that she really wanted to
know and he appreciated her tone. So he ex-
plained, slowly, carefully.

"When I was growing up, see, my parents
wouldn't let me play with other kids. They had
this terrible fear I'd catch pink eye, so they'd

171

only let me out to go to school. One day about nine guys were pounding me in the playground and there *He* was. Right out of the blue."

"You mean Captain Chaos?"

"Yep. Right out of the blue."

"Man!" Pamela thrilled to the idea. "It would be a gas to have a friend like that."

"First you gotta get a mask and a cape."

"Yeah, I know. Maybe something in Tartan plaid. My family's Scottish."

Victor looked at her thoughtfully, measuring her.

"You'd look good in plaid," he decided.

Pamela Glover squeezed his arm, affectionately.

Victor smiled happily and pressed the gas pedal. The ambulance picked up speed, raced on.

J. J. and Dr. Van Helsing slept on.

The rain continued to pelt down, washing down the windshield, flooding the road's shoulder in eddying trickles. But Victor no longer minded.

Captain Chaos would look out for all of them. They were the good guys, too!

* * *

Mad Dog's pickup truck was runing on a two-lane road through the rugged hills of Arizona, north of Prescott. Batman was driving. Their ever faithful and perennially right-hand man, the Law, was racing beside them, siren shrieking. When they reached the crest of a long hill, the road sign announced: ASH FORK 6 MILES. Batman grunted laconically and downbraked for the descent. The heavy GMC lumbered downward. Batman, very mindful of the police patrol car racing to catch up with him, waited until the copper was almost directly alongside him before he leaned from the window and shouted: "No brakes! No brakes!"

Reaction was immediate and exactly what Batman hoped for.

The cop car raced ahead of him, lights flashing, siren keening, jumping ahead to clear any oncoming traffic out of Batman's path. No brakes is never funny—the worst kind of trouble for anything on wheels. Or off them, if it happens to be in the way. Batman began to laugh. Mad Dog smiled appreciatively, then straightened up in his seat.

At the base of the long hill was a railroad grade crossing.

And a freight train was coming. A long, slow line of heavy stock cars and oilers and freight cars. Mad Dog tensed. A train was always a serious threat to any Cannonballer's progress, and he wanted Batman to beat it to the crossing. But Batman was pressing the brakes—gently at first, then he frowned and pressed with more force. Nothing happened. In fact, the GMC was picking up speed, fully gathering up its forward impetus. Batman's brow furrowed. He obviously really had no brakes, and the freight train kept on coming.

Batman, thin-lipped, turned his head toward Mad Dog. "I'd just like to ask you something," he said, casually.

Mad Dog, unconcerned, unknowing, said: "Shoot."

"How long do you reckon it will be before we get to that crossing down there?"

"Oh, I dunno. Maybe ten—fifteen seconds. Why?"

Batman was very calm about it all. "I just thought you might like to take these last few moments to think about your family, all the laughs we've had, and maybe write a will. . . ." And then his voice rose in a blurted shout. "Because we really *don't* have any *goddamn brakes!*"

Mad Dog's eyes finally showed their true color as they flew wide open in disbelief. They were caramel brown.

The GMC hurtled down toward the crossing and the oncoming string of freight cars like a rolling boulder dropping into the Grand Canyon. Batman's skill as a driver was now put to its sternest test. And this was something Mad Dog could not help with at all.

A murderous, thunderous, killing collision was imminent.

Even all thoughts about the Cannonball vanished. Winning or losing was second to the big 'L'—Life!

And now, had Seymour Goldfarb been present, he would have seen a sight to delight his James Bond heart, a spectacle that will forever belong in the pantheon of daredevil, trick driving. In one splendid maneuver of the wheel. The man who thinks fast and moves fast is bound to win over trouble and catastrophe. Batman joined the immortals and saved his own neck into the bargain.

The police car, seeing the train too, had spun off the road into a field, waiting. Batman did not take that route.

He bulleted the runaway truck toward a cattle loading ramp at trackside and, ploughing upward, mounted the tall ramp full throttle and within amazing, flying seconds, propelled the GMC *clear above the height of the passing train,* landing it safely on the far side of the road. With the freight cars clacking behind him, Batman sped on, rushing the GMC down the road.

Any Cannonballer, rival or not, would have cheered too. Except Mad Dog. He took it for granted and clearly had misunderstood all that Batman had tried to tell him.

"Quit kidding around, will you?" Mad Dog said dryly. "Man, for a minute there I thought we were *really* in trouble."

Batman said nothing. They had no brakes but the GMC was still rolling. Time enough later to see to the damn things when they hit the first flat stretch of real estate.

Arizona—Hah! They could give it back to John Wayne!

* * *

The early morning was wearing on, and the adventures and misadventures of the Cannonball competitors continued to pile up. In fact, the entire odyssey across more than three thousand miles of American soil could have filled several large tomes had all the various stories and accounts been tallied up.

Consider what was happening to the young Sheik and his white Rolls Royce. And his worn-out, heavy-weight, pistol-packing bodyguards.

The California border patrol at Blythe had flagged down the speeding, dust-covered Rolls Royce, and the young Sheik had evidently responded to Officer Elkins in the worst possible way. That CHP worthy was writing out a full report on the man with the beard and the white teeth and the flowing *burnoose*.

The two burly bodyguards were no help now. . . .

And they were a sorry sight indeed. Ties undone, suits rumpled and stained, their shirts dirty, stubbles of beard sprouting from unshaven cheeks. Officer Elkin had never been presented with a more outrageous trio in his entire highway patrol life.

As the bodyguards lolled listlessly in the rear of the Rolls, the young Sheik tried to talk his way out American style. He made his voice pleasant, coated with oil, for Officer Elkin's benefit. Surely, such a gentlemanly looking officer would understand!

"Please do not misconstrue my remark about my mother planning to purchase Southern California as an attempt to influence your not giving me a ticket, officer. I am sure she will still consider keeping you on as a member of the Highway Patrol—" The Sheik smiled winningly. "Regardless of how shabbily you treated her son."

Officer Elkin kept hold of the Sheik's license, turning it round and round as though trying to get a bead on it.

Like the Sheik himself, it was weird, and incoherently Arabic. He could not even tell which end was up. Finally, defeated, he pocketed it, smiled back at the young Sheik, showing his *own* teeth, for a change.

"You might want to tell that to the judge," Officer Elkin said.

The white Rolls Royce was grounded. Temporarily, at least.

The bodyguards took it lying down, so to speak. Not so the young Sheik.

He began to rant, rave, walk around in circles and call upon Allah for divine intervention. None was forthcoming. Allah was obviously busy, elsewhere.

Officer Elkin had the last say. "You're in America now. Cut all the lingo, and that's an order! You're giving me an earache!"

The Law had spoken.

Man arranges, Life rearranges. How else to

explain the sudden presence of a construction site in the very path of the Cannonballers?

Later that morning, at a construction site along the main road, a working crew labored with the implantment of a pipeline. All traffic, coming and going, was temporarily blocked. And that managed to include the gleaming red Ferrari, the bullet-nosed black Lamborghini, the sleekly silver Aston-Martin, the heavy GMC pickup truck, the finally-on-the-right-road Subaru, the motorbiking JUST MARRIEDS, and, happily, the white ambulance.

The bogus Fathers Blake and Fenderbaum.

Marcie Thatcher and Jill Rivers in their form-fitting coveralls.

Seymour Goldfarb and but one more beautiful dame.

Mad Dog and Batman, brakes in good order.

The Japanese driving team. Driver-San Numbers One and Two, still smugly sure of victory.

Bradford W. Compton and Shakey Finch, who were taking advantage of the jam, refreshing themselves at the gas station across the way.

And J. J. McClure, Victor, Pamela Glover and Dr. Nicholas Van Helsing. And Captain Chaos, of course. In spirit, at least.

The gang was all there and a construction boss informed all within earshot that the ". . . *road'll be open in five minutes, folks . . ."*

Father Jamie Blake was not unhappy with the announcement. He had spotted the white ambulance and was just a little anxious to settle a few matters with J. J. McClure. He and feisty Fenderbaum had had to do a lot of hard talking to square themselves with that cop back there who thought he was bringing in a couple of armed and dangerous, highway-robber child molesters. He was almost smiling as he strolled through the knot of varied vehicles to address J. J. McClure. His shoulders were squared and his arms swung loosely at his sides.

J. J. saw him coming and waited.

"Well, well!" Jamie Blake smiled up at him. "If it isn't Albert Schweitzer. Thanks for all those nice things you said about us in Missouri. Hope you didn't do anything besides blow your engine."

"Just trying to return the favor," J. J. agreed, amiably, "that your little pint-of-shit sidekick did for us in Ohio."

"I wouldn't talk. It looks like you're riding around with the Goodyear Blimp." His smile at Victor was more than direct.

J. J. opened the door of the ambulance and started out, angrily. No one could pick on Victor while he was around. "Oh, yeah? Listen. One more wise-assed remark out of you and I'm gonna stuff your rosary beads in your ear."

Jamie Blake lost his smile. His eyes went dead and his lips thinned. Softly he said; "You're welcome to try but I've got a piece of advice."

"Yeah, what's that?"

"Bring friends."

The construction tie-up was getting on every-

179

body's nerves, and seemed a helluva lot longer than a mere five minutes. Unfortunate, in light of the forthcoming events—the fight, the trouble, would not have happened otherwise. Just lay it to Fate, which always kicks every man and every woman right in the seat of the pants sooner or later, when they least expect it.

* * *

A band of Hell's Angels—that leather-jacketed breed of short-vested, bearded, sun-glassed troublemakers—now came thundering up the road to the gas station across from the construction site in a blare of sirens, motors, catcalls and shouts like a herd of half-crazed mechanical buffalo.

But buffalo don't wage war, and these dudes were thoroughly prepared. The emblems and symbols were all in evidence: death-heads and swastikas rampant, crash helmets adorned with every kind of *Screw You* logo there was. One lead bike bore a flying pennant that proclaimed to the watching world that DRACULA SUCKS!

Unluckily, Bradford W. Compton, creased trousers and all, and Shakey Finch, fake blond wig and all, caught the eye of the leader of these galoots who considered homosexuals and working for a living two of the worst ills visited upon Mankind.

The lead bikeman, somewhere south of Brando and north of Lee Marvin, halted on his chopper and regarded Compton and Finch with the sort of interest a hawk has for a chicken. He dismounted gleefully, and sidled over to Bradford W. Compton. The other bikemen, their own choppers stilled, paid close attention. The fun was about to begin. Finch's blond wig and Compton's expensive business suit were honey for hungry bees.

"Hey, man!" The lead biker smirked. "That's really precious, you ridin' around in that cute little wig."

Shakey Finch's face looked like one of his pizzas. He knotted up, and bunched his fists but Bradford W. Compton, the voice of reason, intervened.

"Just a little joke," he *hah-hahed*, crisply enough. "We aren't really that way."

The leader was not convinced. Or through. He spread his hands and ran them over Compton's superb business suit.

"And ain't he dressed up like a regular little gentleman! That genuine gray flannel suit. Superthreads!"

Before Compton could respond in kind, the chief bikeman had grabbed at him, tugging a vest pocket and ripping it off the suit with one vicious, downward swipe.

The tension was building now. Electricity was in the air.

Bradford W. Compton was abruptly very nervous. His smile was a pale ghost of his former

181

coolness.

"The best!" he shrilled. "Straight from Brooks Brothers. And this tie—raw silk!"

With that, he whipped out a small penknife, slashed off his own tie with one swift slice and handed it over to the biker. "Here—you might want to complete your ensemble."

Everybody hooted and laughed. The chief bikeman now growled low in his throat. His cruel face twisted with rage. His gimlet eyes showed savagery. He took a meaningful step toward Bradford W. Compton. Shakey Finch tensed, fists still knotted. The Pizza King could smell a fight from nine miles away. This looked like the goods.

"Forget it," the bikeman said, dropping the tie to the stained concrete drive of the gas station. "I'm gonna take something else that's yours, instead." A huge, bald biking giant eased up to his side.

Bradford W. Compton *hah-hahed* again like a regular fellow. "What's that?"

"Your ass!" the bikeman roared. And came at him, arms windmilling, fists pumping. Shakey Finch sprang forward, a cry of rage erupting from his throat. The battle royal was on.

Bradford W. Compton slammed over backward as the bikeman's ugly knuckle sandwich thundered into his jaw. Shakey Finch, lending a fist, swung a roundhouse right, with all his beef behind it, and the king of these Hell's Angels, admittedly caught offguard, suddenly found himself smacking back into a cold, hard gasoline pump. That was all the rest of them needed. Scrambling and leaping from their bikes, they plunged into the heart of the melee. Someone yelled *"Geronimo!"* and Shakey Finch cried out *"Holy Pepperoni!"* as a ton of converging bodies hit him. He went down under a squad of toe-stomping, shit-kicking, good old-fashioned hoodlums. Bradford W. Compton, rebounding masterfully, stumbled back into the fray. With only half a tie and one remaining vest pocket—and a tire iron he had found somewhere—he swung about, as well as any D'Artagnan had ever wielded a bludgeon. Bikemen howled left and right as the iron hit home, and suddenly, portly Shakey Finch was reemerging from the pile of bodies, his blond wig thoroughly askew, one eye glazing over in the middle of a spreading bruise. But the thrill of a good fight kept him going.

The battle raged, oil cans scattered, windows crackled and rang as they broke.

Meanwhile, amidst the pack of stalled vehicles, J. J. McClure and Jamie Blake stood squared off and ready to swing.

Just then, the commotion at the gas station across the way captured their attention. They turned in unison and in awe as the lead biker staggered from his resting place at the base of the pump and, drunken from the blows received, tried to spearhead a rally against the weakening flank of two. For the fighting Finch and courageous Compton were, after all, two middle-aged businessmen, no match for a ferocious phalanx of bikers.

"You guys gonna help?" He gestured across the roadway at the developing battle. Bodies struggled, squirmed, twisted. Bikes toppled. voices yelled.

"Why should we?" Jamie Blake shrugged. "That road opens and you're long gone. Why don't *you* go help? You're the Good Samaritan."

"Yeah, Sam," Morris Fenderbaum laughed wickedly. "Go do your own *schtick,* man!"

J. J. controlled his rising anger.

"No way. You guys aren't getting out of my sight."

Too late. Matters were taken out of J. J.'s hands. He should have known—or at least guessed—that Captain Chaos would not sit unperturbed in the very midst of such an uneven, cruel fray. Two against ten. Ten against two!

And when the fierce shout rose in the morning air, J. J. did not have to turn around. Only one hero could yell like that. *Captain Chaos* himself. In person.

Victor—or rather, the masked defender—was running past J. J. and the Ferrari priests, weaving among the stalled vehicles, virtually flying across the roadway. Cape aflutter, cowl mask in place, face scrunched up and determined, the pudgy mechanic was transformed.

He seemed taller, wider, shoulders bigger—awesome, somehow.

Then, he was in the very thick of it, arms

thrusting, body whirling like a top. From each thrust and whirl, the limp figure of a biker seemed to fly out like a rag doll.

Still, bikemen are resilient so-and-sos. The fallen rag dolls got up again and Captain Chaos soon disappeared from view, lost in a welter of tackling Hell's Angels. J. J. sighed and started across the road.

Victor needed help—no matter what.

The priests watched as J. J. McClure waded into the scrap. A shout went up. Not far behind were the Fathers Blake and Fenderbaum.

Soon enough, it was no longer a contest between the bikemen and Bradford W. Compton and Shakey Finch. And the duel-to-the-death competitive air of the Sea-To-Shining-Sea Memorial Trophy Dash melted like so much ice in the California desert. It was one for all now—the *Cannon caballeros* would stick it out together. *Camaraderie* survived the simple fact that only one vehicle could win the race that all were engaged in.

Seymour Goldfarb rose smoothly and efficiently from the wheel of his silvery Aston-Martin, excused himself from his new lady, and loped easily across the road.

The Japanese saw their chance to participate in a real, American free-for-all, and lost no time skittering across the road, their *kamikaze* scarves waving just like Old Glory at Fort McHenry.

The Battle of the Gas Station was now in full

fly. The Cannonball was forgotten, at least for a little while. Pamela Glover and Dr. Nicholas Van Helsing felt like cheering—which they promptly did!

* * *

The deciding gimmick, the one factor that made it go the way of the good guys, was the extraordinary fighting skills of the two Japanese Subaru drivers. They made Bruce Lee look like just another victim of St. Vitus' dance. They were both so superb in the martial arts that all others in the fight were soon bystanders.

Seymour Goldfarb, in particular, was of no use whatsoever, poor man. Not even resembling Roger Moore could help him here. He had only had time enough to posture briefly, hands cocked in the approved *karate* style, when the bald-headed hulk ducked under his guard and knocked him flat on his backside with a hard haymaker. Seymour Goldfarb saw no more combat that day.

J. J. and Victor between them accounted for a couple of the bikers, but their punches and blows seemed like flyswatters against the Hell's Angels. The knockout punch was missing. Ditto for the Fathers. Blake and Fenderbaum were good scrappers, street-smart, back-alley fighters.

But still it took the Japanese team to write *finis* to the scene. And their signature was an assortment of kicks and shoves and tosses that completely wrecked the black-leathered meanies. It was the Land of the Rising Sun's proudest Cannonball moment thus far.

The Japanese team was trying to revive Hell's Angels members, apparently with the intention of giving them another drubbing, when the roadblock was suddenly lifted.

The priests were the first to break for their racer, sprinting madly over fallen bodies to their red Ferrari.

Seymour Goldfarb, awake again, made for his silvery beauty, coolly smoothing his mussed hair as he went.

The girls in the black Lamborghini were already roaring off, cheered on by the construction workers, who waved and whistled their approval of such feminine excellence of face and figure and force.

Bradford W. Compton and Shakey Finch, bloody but unbowed, were remounting their overweighted motorcycle.

And J. J. McClure and Captain Chaos, Just Plain Victor again, were desperately scrambling for the white ambulance.

Mad Dog and Batman, who had laid back from the fight, watching it with amusement from their GMC, had followed the Lamborghini in crossing through the opened block.

J. J. McClure tried not to swear as he whipped the ambulance in gear. Victor, folding his Captain Chaos costume, was all sweat and shine, convinced again that Good *will* triumph over Evil. Lovely Pamela Glover and grim Dr. Nicholas Van Helsing swallowed their felicitations. They had begun to get a small idea of what, exactly, this race meant to J. J. Mc Clure and Victor—just about *everything*.

"I'm with you, J. J. And you too, Victor." Pamela Glover sang out her vote of confidence. Dr. Van Helsing nodded.

J. J. McClure smiled grimly and floored the gas pedal.

The white ambulance shot away clear, taking up the trail of the black Lamborghini, the silvery Aston-Martin, the GMC and the red Ferrari. Behind him, Bradford W. Compton's motorcycle was blasting into action with a helluva roar.

The Cannonball was on again, this time for keeps! Somebody was going to win all the marbles, and J. J. McClure wanted it to be no one but him—and Victor. And Pamela Glover, who had crept into his heart like magic. And even Dr. Nicholas Van Helsing. He had grown quite fond of the wall-eyed faker.

BURNING RUBBER

Time was running out.

All the vehicles had been on the road better
than twenty-four hours. The endless miles and
stretches of macadam, the country roads and
vast interstates, the cities and towns and wide
places in the road—all were just a mad montage
of signs, directions and roadmarkers. And the
omnipresent Law . . . in the form of patrol cars,
motorcycles and officers, had also been hell on
wheels. Victor and J. J. McClure both felt as if
they had been living a nightmare of oil and gas
and rotten sandwiches and a hundred pints of
black coffee and thin beer. All the jams and
scrapes and hairy situations, like this last mad
romp at the gas station back there, all for what?
J. J. McClure could feel his nerves wearing raw.

Which was why Victor was driving again. J. J.
was trying to think, to come up with something.
They still had not tagged the Lamborghini, the
Ferrari or the Aston-Martin, and the race did
not look too good, right now. J. J. McClure was
a very worried man.

"Goddammit, Victor! Move it! Those jerks will be long gone!"

Pamela Glover, who was really into the race now, backed up J. J.'s order. "C'mon, Victor, c'mon baby. Drive it like you stole it!"

Dr. Van Helsing hollered from the rear. "Yes, man. Go, man, go. And all that."

J. J. looked at Victor and bit his lower lip.

"Victor, get *him*. We need his help."

Victor seemed troubled at this request. "I don't know where he is. He ain't around."

"But we *need* him, Victor," Pamela thrust in, pleading.

J. J. frowned. "Why did you take off the mask?"

"*I* didn't take off the mask," Victor protested. "*He* took off his own mask."

"Whatever," J. J. snapped. "But we need him now. He's our only hope. You can see that, can't you, Victor?"

"He must be out there somewhere," Victor sighed, unhappy that he could not oblige his dearest friend on all this earth. "I sure hope he isn't mad at us."

J. J. raised his voice, as if talking to a child. He was firmer, louder. "Get him! Right now!"

Dr. Van Helsing help up and extended his faithful hypodermic needle. "Will this help?"

"Forget it, Doc," J. J. said softly and then returned his attention to Victor. "Now! I want him now!"

"I can't!" Victor moaned, unhappily.

J. J. was not himself. His hands shot out and

grabbed Victor by the fat throat. "Goddammit, we want him! Now!"

Pamela, with surprising strength, pulled J. J. away from Victor. Her eyes were uncommonly sensible and sane.

"J. J., for God's sake, it's not Victor's fault if Captain Chaos isn't around. He may be helping one of his other friends. Other people need him too, you know."

J. J. released Victor. But his fury had not subsided. His darkly handsome face was suffused with anger. Right now, he was upset with everybody and everything. Including Pamela Glover.

"I don't give a damn if he's on a benefit tour for the March of Dimes! He isn't here and that's all I care about!"

Angrily, J. J. scrambled out of the front seat, sweeping by Pamela Glover and landing in the back section of the ambulance. He jerked a bottle of Coke out of the cooler there. Within him, the rage was ebbing but the drums of defeat were sounding all the louder.

They all looked like losers now. All four of them! They could never win the Cannonball unless—

His heart pounded wildly, the blood thundered in his veins.

For from the front seat, where Victor sat at the wheel, came a blasting, bold and brazen voice, breaking the silence. A familiar voice whose booming tone was like money from the folks, money in the bank—or just plain found money.

Victor had spoken—loudly and clearly and unmistakably—the old heart-warming war cry. The cry of the great hero, the mighty warrior, the foe of all Evil everywhere. The caped crusader himself.

Captain Chaos had come back! In addition to his superstrength and skills, the Captain was a fool for speed. He drove better than any man alive! J. J. McClure felt like singing as he swallowed his Coke.

Yea, Team!

* * *

Meanwhile, back at the gas station, bikers lay sprawled everywhere. Only the Japanese were on their feet.

One of them was pouring water on a fallen warrior, while Driver Number Two was patting the unconscious face awake. With this teamwork, both men were able to persuade the dazed combatant to stand again. Instantly, both Judo-flopped him back to obliviion.

But now it looked like the lark had given up its last entertaining note. The Subaru team conferred briefly in Nipponese. One of them was really insistent. Translated, his feelings were:

"See if you can wake up a few more. I'd rather do this any day compared to running that

idiot race."

Which probably explains why the well-equipped Subaru would not finish in the money. Not even the Cannonball Memorial Dash Trophy Race could compete with martial arts for excitement, as far as these fellows were concerned.

* * *

The white ambulance, a creamy blur on the Los Angeles freeway, wove and darted in and out of traffic. Onlookers would presume that a maniac was at the wheel. Not so. It was Captain Chaos, who knew no fear and acknowledged no speed limits and/or traffic signs. The lawman did not live who could stop such a man or such a vehicle. J. J. McClure's prayers had been answered.

J. J.'s simple plan worked like magic, for with siren blasting and red lights flashing, everybody made room for the ambulance, that vehicle of mercy, including the Los Angeles Police Department.

It was clear sailing all the way.

"Oh, J. J.," Pamela Glover marveled. "I think we're going to win! I feel it in my bones."

"Uh huh. You're thinking of the trees again, aren't you?"

"How did you know?"

"Too easy. Every time you feel good, you think of those trees and laying under them on a moonlit night and—"

Pamela Glover's eyes shone. She moistened her lips, "There's one thing you don't know, J. J., and it makes all the difference there can be. All the difference in the world."

"And what's that?"

"I'm always with somebody under the trees," Pamela Glover said, with a funny catch in her voice. "And *now* that somebody always has your face. You know what I mean?"

J. J. McClure grinned, happily.

Dr. Van Helsing started to sing again.

"Redondo Beach . . . here we come . . . right back where we . . ."

Nobody minded his terrible voice at all. Everybody had a song in his or her heart. The Cannonball was winding down to the finish now, and it looked like the white ambulance had as good a chance as any. How could they have guessed that Fate was about to intercede again? Old Big Nose himself. And yet—who knows? Maybe Fate really is a *woman*.

* * *

The final entrants were now dicing their way through the Los Angeles traffic. And now they all began to see signs and markers that said the

Portofino Inn was but a few miles away. The end of the Cannonball Memorial Dash Trophy Race was literally in sight, the grueling contest that had been run from sea to shining sea.

If the race was to the swiftest, these were indeed the *crème de la crème*.

The bullet-nosed black Lamborghini.

The silvery Aston-Martin.

The gleaming red Ferrari.

The sturdy GMC pickup truck.

The solitary motorcycle.

And, of course, the white ambulance.

The white Rolls Royce, the PDRA panel truck, and the ugly gray stock car of Stan Barrett and David Pearson had all been scratched along the way. One by too much mad speed and Arabian high-handedness, and the other two by the long, avenging arm of Arthur J. Foyt of the Highway Safety Enforcement Unit of the National Highway Traffic Safety Administration. Three cheers for Arthur J. Foyt.

Marcie Thatcher and Jill Rivers grinned broadly at each other, their shining faces alive with anticipation of victory.

Seymour Goldfarb calmly smoked, his keen eyes fixed on the distant goal. Yet, even Goldfarb felt the pitter-patter of a thrill in his soul. Poised beside him an Angels momma, the hard-looking chopper woman he had picked up during the gas station imbroglio, smoked a cigar at his side.

Fathers Jamie Blake and Morris Fenderbaum were mentally collecting their championship, envisioning the chagrin of the Greek when he had to pay off a losing bet.

Driving hard and ruthlessly, as per their custom, Mad Dog and Batman had the hammer down all the way.

Bradford W. Compton and Shakey Finch clung to each other on their two-wheeled tornado. Finch's blond wig flapped in the breeze.

Victor, alias Captain Chaos, was in full ascension. And J. J. McClure, Pamela Glover and Dr. Nicholas Van Helsing were with him in spirit as well as body.

The mad, motoring cavalcade moved as one body, tailgating each other, crowding the roadway, thrusting forward with thundering engines and dizzying turns of their wheels.

Everything in front of them got out of the way.

The time clock was running, too. It never stops.

The record was being threatened—the time record of thirty-two hours and fifty-one minutes set by Heinz and Yarborough in that other wild and glorious Memorial Trophy Dash Race.

Suddenly, the Portofino Inn burst into view. The Pacific Ocean shimmered to the left. Redondo Beach. The overhead sun blazed down. The crowds, waiting expectantly, roared.

The fastest cars in the Cannonball zoomed toward the finish. This, at long last, was It.

The End.

Finis.

Showdown.
When one car would get all the marbles.
But which one?

* * *

A vast, roaring mob of machinery was now descending on the parking lot gate of the Portofino Inn with all systems go.

The small booth at the gate was manned by a laconic California surfer serenely leafing through a battered copy of *Rolling Stone*. The concert of engine roar and pound reached his ears and he looked up.

He blanched in disbelief and dropped the magazine, and back-pedaled out of harm's way. The Cannonball had dropped in at his front door.

Mad Dog's pickup truck and the Suzuki slammed through the gate side by side. Directly behind them rushed the Lamborghini, the Ferrari, the Aston-Martin and the ambulance. It was a scene from a motor maniac's nightmare, filled with howling engines, blasting horns and the stench of scorched rubber.

Mad Dog spun the wheel sharply, making the hard-right turn into the very last stretch of open ground. In doing so, he came to unexpected and dazzling grief. The coolly taciturn Batman for once cried out in despair and shock.

The truck spun out, wheels whirling wildly, and came to a full dead stop, blocking the roadway. No vehicle was going anywhere now. The GMC was the last roadblock, and no one could go around it.

Realizing that the last few desperate yards to the all-important finish line was blocked, all the crews of all the trapped follow-up vehicles reacted to a man—and woman—spontaneously, and with no regard for appearances, rhyme or reason.

Everybody bailed out of their machines like wind-up toys and sprang for the hotel lobby, each clutching his or her time card. The great Cannonball contest had degenerated into the oldest contest since Adam took off after Eve—a foot race.

Marcie Thatcher, Jill Rivers, Mad Dog, Batman, Seymour Goldfarb, Bradford W. Compton, Shakey Finch, Fathers Jamies Blake and Morris Fenderbaum, each and all, were sprinting madly for pay dirt.

And lo, Victor, *Captain Chaos*, led all the rest!

J. J. Mc Clure, at the outset, had thrown a savage body block in the best football tradition that cleaned out half the field. He bowled over all the males with a desperate surge of his athletic body, slowing them down considerably. Only Marcie Thatcher eluded him. She darted out and was right on Victor's flying heels, her form-fitted, coveralled figure making great time.

J. J. watched from where he lay, slapping the ground enthusiastically, urging Victor on to victory.

And Fate intervened—blast him. Or rather *Her!*

A forlorn woman, standing on the pier of the nearby marina, at the Inn's very door, began to scream hysterically. There was no mistaking the anguish of her voice, nor the import of her cry:

"HELP, HELP! MY BABY IS DROWNING!"

Victor heard that cry. That is to say, Captain Chaos did. He stopped running dead in his tracks. His body began to twitch, to quiver. His shoulders arched.

"Victor!" J. J. bellowed, his heart six feet under, "Keep going! Get to the clock, goddammit!"

Marcie Thatcher flashed by his stock-still figure, heels flying.

Victor was already running the other way, veering toward the screaming woman and her drowning baby. Captain Chaos knew his duty when he saw it. And Humanity was his most precious charge.

Which cost J. J. McClure the Cannonball.

Marcie Thatcher was racing into the lobby, waving time card, triumphantly punching in. Winning the Cannonball Memorial Trophy Dash, the Sea-To-Shining-Sea competition. Nobody else was even close. They had the fastest time.

J. J. McClure collapsed in bitter frustration, among the pile of contestants now reduced to that highly forgettable position of Also-Ran. The bitter gall of defeat and failure was difficult to swallow.

Meanwhile, Captain Chaos was emerging from the salty sea, clambering onto the dock, carrying the rescued 'baby' that his heroism and strength and courage had returned to its mother's arms. Only the 'baby' was a small, shivering poodle! A dog! The grateful owner fell all over the Captain, kissing him with tears of gratitude. Victor was wet and beaming. Onlookers were cheering and applauding. He strode majestically back to where J. J. McClure lay. In the lobby of the Portofino, Marcie Thatcher was taking all her bows and kudos. Jill Rivers had joined her. The ladies embraced each other and thumped each other on the back.

But J. J. McClure rose from the earth like a storm cloud.

Victor stood before him, sheepish now, holding on to his wet cape and dripping mask. Pamela Glover and Dr. Nicholas Van Helsing hovered close by. But not too close . . .

"Goddammit, Victor!" The confirmation belonged to J. J. alone—he had earned it the hard way. "We were winners. Winners! Do you understand that? And you go and pull that idiot stunt. I have had it. Had it! Do you understand what I am saying? I have had it with this Captain Chaos bullshit once and for all. . . ."

Victor could say nothing. He looked almost contrite. But under the contrition, something was stirring. You could see it in his little black eyes.

J. J. tore the mask and cape from him and flung them down. He began to stomp up and down on them, grinding them into the dirt. Then he picked them up and began to rip, violently. When the shredding job was complete, he was panting. He flung the pieces at Victor's feet. His rage had run its course.

"There! That's the end of Captain Chaos. What do you think of that?"

Victor's smile had spread from his eyes to his whole face.

"It's okay by me, J. J." he wheezed. "Because, if you want to know the truth, I mean—I've always dreamed of being *Captain Crusader!*"

J. J. McClure's handsome jaw dropped. He was speechless.

Victor whipped out a brand new cape and another cowled mask and was donning them quickly, whistling a little off key. He posed, hands on hips, and strutted back and forth. J. J. shook his head and then began to laugh.

The Cannonball defeat began to fade.

J. J. pulled Victor to him in a big bear hug, laughing from deep down. Victor hugged back, beaming like a Jack-o'-Lantern. Pamela Glover joined in, and J. J. kissed her. Even Dr. Nicholas Van Helsing beamed his approval, looking on, clinging to his crooked and rusty hypodermic needle. He looked a little more like Dr. Jekyll and a little less like Mr. Hyde now.

Happiness can do that to people.

Behind them, more cars, more machinery were still rolling in. The wreck of the GMC had been cleared away. More Cannonballers, losers all, were trickling in. The truckers, the stock cars with the PRDA's intact and even the late-running Japanese team. The last to arrive was a cab, which pulled in swiftly and urgently.

From this noncompeting vehicle emerged the one, the only Arthur J. Foyt. He fairly lurched from the machine, eyes popping, face contorted in righteous disgust. The Cannonball spectacle truly sickened his rationalistic soul. Such nonsense! Such waste! Such stupidity!

Foyt was fairly crazed with anger. He strode up to J. J. McClure and friends, and began to waggle an accusing finger. Seymour Goldfarb, more impeccable than anyone in that race had a right to be, had drifted over to the group. Clinging to his tailored sleeve was the cigar-packing chopper momma. Goldfarb's tuxedo stripes gleamed in the sunlight.

"You, you . . . Visigoths!" Arthur J. Foyt roared, frazzled and still furious. "How do you feel after you've raped the American highways?"

J. J. smiled. "Absolutely terrific. In fact, we were just talking about turning around and racing back to Darien."

"You'll have to drive over my dead, mutilated body to do it!"

Seymour Goldfarb rose to the occasion. Coolness was called for. "I say, old man, you're beginning to lose your grip. Here, have one of my cigars. I have them especially made for me by this Cuban I know—a fugitive from the Castro regime—"

He had opened his silver case, offering one to Foyt.

Foyt shook his head. "I never touch the things—" Then, he paused. "But what the hell. We've broken every other rule of human decency. Why not?"

"Why not, indeed?" Roger Moore Goldfarb purred.

Foyt took the cigar shakily and stuffed it between his lips. He began to pat his pockets for a match. J. J. McClure looked at Seymour Goldfarb. Goldfarb smiled, knowingly.

"Mr. Foyt? Please," he murmured. "Feel free to use the lighter in my car."

Foyt grunted, dove into the passenger seat of the Aston-Martin and punched the lighter button on the dashboard.

Seymour Goldfarb winked at J. J., Victor, Pamela Glover and Dr. Nicholas Van Helsing. Then he watched Foyt pull the lighter out, light the cigar and begin to puff. Seymour Goldfarb was floored.

Nothing had happened! Not the expected, at least. Frowning, he too climbed into the Aston-Martin.

He stared at Arthur J. Foyt, puzzled.

Foyt was puffing away, enjoying the cigar.

Enjoying *something* for a change. Seymour Goldfarb took the dashboard lighter from Foyt, turning it over in his fingers, examining it. Could Q have failed?

Oh, well. There was a first time for everything.

Sighing in disappointment, Seymour Goldfarb inserted the lighter back into the dashboard. *C'est la guerre* and all that.

There was a loud report.

It might have been heard all the way back to M's office in London. The sky was, now, the limit!

The roof of the Aston-Martin had jettisoned, and Arthur J. Foyt and Seymour Goldfarb were catapulted from the car, up, up, up—then down, down, down, until they splashed with a distant 'cloop' into the nearby ocean.

There were a few tense moments while the hushed crowd searched the watery horizon. Then two heads appeared—Seymour Goldfarb and Arthur J. Foyt began to swim back for shore, using long easy strokes. A cheer went up.

J. J. chuckled. "I always knew that Foyt was all wet."

Pamela Glover squeezed his arm, eyes shining. Victor clapped.

Fathers Blake and Fenderbaum laughed out loud, too, even though the thought of the huge sum of money lost to the Greek was galling.

Bradford W. Compton and Shakey Finch were even resigned about the whole thing. "Win one, lose one," Bradford W. Compton said, and Shakey Finch loosened the belt of his trousers, heaving a long sigh.

Mad Dog and Batman lit up cigarillos and puffed like *grandees*. The black man poked his partner in the ribs and reflected, "Wish we hadn't run out of joints but these ain't half bad."

The race was done. Finished, ended, *kaput*. Now, it was time to celebrate.

A giant party was in the offing at the Portofino Inn. Winners and losers all would unite in one big, free-swinging, fun-having grand *soirée*, the devil take tomorrow! And the next race, wherever that might be. Whatever that might be. Whenever it might be.

* * *

"Do you like trees?" J. J. McClure asked Pamela Glover in a quiet moment later on, when the moon was riding high and the palm trees along the Redondo shore were waving gently in an off-shore breeze. Behind them, the party was going full blast. Music and joy and laughter and singing could be heard in equal muted measure.

"Sure I like trees," Pamela whispered.

"Me, too. I think they're great," J. J. said softly.

"What do you like best about them?"

J. J. Mc Clure smiled. "What I like best about them—is the way you can lay under them and—" He paused, as if searching for the right word.

"And?" she prompted. "Go on. You're doing just fine."

J. J. said not a word more. He did not have to. He took Pamela Glover in his arms, and began to show her exactly what he meant about trees.

Maybe they had won the biggest Race there is—Love; and then again, maybe—Life: the two best rides of all.

THE END

EXPENSIVE PLEASURES
By Stephen Lewis

PRICE: $2.95

LB929

CATEGORY: Novel

WHAT HAPPENS WHEN A WOMAN'S *EVERY* FANTASY COMES TRUE?

Cara fulfilled her wildest dreams as a superstar model. But she wanted more, and indulged in one more fantasy—to succeed as a fashion designer. Her inspired designs and transcontinental romances carried her to the apex of the fashion industry and high society. But behind her public smile hid the private pain of lovers lost in a world of diamond-studded decadence, sexual abandon, and betrayal. Soon, everyone wore her designer jeans and envied her extravagant lifestyle. But would all her fantasies come true? Would the high risks be worth those EXPENSIVE PLEASURES....A sizzling novel from the author of THE REGULARS and THE BEST SELLERS.

THOROUGHBREDS
By Michael Geller

PRICE: $2.75   LB901
CATEGORY: Novel

GREED, WEALTH AND LUST WERE A WINNING COMBINATION!

High society's lovers, gamblers, movers and shakers all flocked to the glamorous and exciting $1 million winner-take-all race of the century —the fabulous Superstakes! Everyone had something to win. They were all THOROUGHBREDS!